THE DAILY

JANE
AUSTEN

A YEAR OF

QUOTES

Edited and with a Foreword by
DEVONEY LOOSER

The University of Chicago Press ✳ *Chicago and London*

The University of Chicago Press, Chicago 60637
The University of Chicago Press, Ltd., London
© 2019 by The University of Chicago
Published 2019
Printed in the United States of America

28 27 26 25 24 23 22 21 20   2 3 4 5

ISBN-13: 978-0-226-65544-4 (paper)
ISBN-13: 978-0-226-65558-1 (e-book)
DOI: https://doi.org/10.7208/chicago/9780226655581.001.0001

Quotes used by permission of Oxford University Press and
Cambridge University Press. See page 198.

Library of Congress Cataloging-in-Publication Data

Names: Looser, Devoney, 1967– editor.
Title: The daily Jane Austen : a year of quotes / edited and with
    a foreword by Devoney Looser.
Description: Chicago ; London : The University of Chicago
    Press, 2019. | Includes index.
Identifiers: LCCN 2019006642 | ISBN 9780226655444 (pbk. : alk.
    paper) | ISBN 9780226655581 (e-book)
Subjects: LCSH: Austen, Jane, 1775–1817—Quotations.
Classification: LCC PR4037 .D355 2019 | DDC 823/.7—dc23
LC record available at https://lccn.loc.gov/2019006642

♾ This paper meets the requirements of ANSI/NISO Z39.48-1992
(Permanence of Paper).

Foreword

It is a truth universally acknowledged that you could put almost anything in the second half of this sentence, because the first half sounds clever and wise and must remind readers of the genius of Jane Austen. Those first six words that form the beginning of *Pride and Prejudice* (1813)—"It is a truth universally acknowledged"—have acquired astonishing literary and cultural power. They kick off one of the most famous beginnings in the history of fiction, if not in all of literature. That's no small feat, with stiff competition from Charles Dickens's "It was the best of times, it was the worst of times," Vladimir Nabokov's "Lolita, light of my life, fire of my loins. My sin, my soul," and Herman Melville's "Call me Ishmael." In the early twenty-first century, however, Austen seems to have overtaken these figures, emerging as the classic novelist responsible for the genre's *most* recognizable opening.

That one line has come to stand in for all of Austen just as emphatically as bonnets, afternoon tea, and the BBC's back catalog. Reasonable people may disagree about whether she deserves her current stature—or this sort of stereotyping. Still, you'd have a hard time arguing that she doesn't warrant the attention. These compulsively repeated, repeatable words secure her fame and circulate in all the best traditional literary places, from print editions to stage adaptations and feature films, not to mention a seemingly endless supply of mugs and T-shirts. Her stories and characters have elbowed their way in to new media, too, with manga, vlogs, and rearview-mirror air fresheners. (My acknowledged truth is that I treasure the "sensibly scented" cardboard Austen that hangs in my car, just as others embrace their dashboard Jesus, fuzzy dice, or mud-flap girls.)

Austen got in on the literary and commercial ground floor of the early nineteenth century. Her words came to proliferate not only in their original and adapted forms but as jokes and slogans. She's our most visible author at the intersection of high-culture credibility and pop-culture cool. This is despite the fact that, with digital printing, any quote or image can now end up on anything. For those of us who savor her every last word, the quip that may best apply here is from *Persuasion*: "How quick come the reasons for approving what we like!" We celebrate her fiction for its matchless heroines, worthy heroes, romance, irony, social criticism, and humor, which is as it should be. We also revere her as an exceptionally gifted writer on the level of the sentence. Even in small, double-digit word-bits, her dialogue crackles, her satire provokes, her humor sings, and her narration is masterful. It's not just that her bons mots are beautifully crafted; they're also crafty.

Just look at that famous opening line in full: "It is a truth universally acknowledged, that a single man in possession of a good fortune, must be in want of a wife." There's poetry in it, with a singsong cadence, consonance (*single, possession, must*), and alliteration (*want, wife*). Its meaning isn't easy to pin down. Notice that there's no assertion that it's flat-out correct; it is only purported to be so by unnamed acknowledgers. The tone is neither obviously straightforward nor positively tongue-in-cheek. The sentiment could be read as true, partly true, or untrue, whether in the world of the novel alone or in the world beyond it. There's so much packed into that single sentence.

But the deft skill and ubiquity of *Pride and Prejudice*'s first sentence also has a downside. It has loomed so large in the practice of quoting her that it muscles out many other excellent lines. That's a loss indeed. Scores of gems of her wit and wisdom deserve to be just as well known, from *Northanger Abbey* on its heroine ("if adventures will not befal a young lady in her own village, she must seek them abroad") to *Persuasion* from its hero ("You pierce my soul. I am half agony, half hope."). Even those lines we *think* we know well deserve greater scrutiny. You may already be aware that Austen described her own writing as like a "little bit (two Inches wide) of Ivory," but did you know that it's a line embedded in a joke about plagiarism and literary theft? You might have been told that Austen coined the term "base ball," in the early chapters of *Northanger Abbey*, but that's actually been debunked. For years, the *Oxford English Dictionary* claimed it was so, but with the arrival of full-text, searchable databases, earlier examples were discovered.

That technology has made it possible to see new things in Austen's word choice and turns of phrase. In *Nabokov's Favorite Word Is Mauve: What the Numbers Reveal about the Classics, Bestsellers, and Our Own Writing*, Ben Blatt credits Austen with being the only writer in his data set who never wrote a book that used "he" more often than "she." That's a fascinating comparative insight, as we try to decide why Austen's well-regarded fiction is sometimes celebrated (or dismissed) as "chick lit." Blatt says Austen's novels also employ a comparatively lower percentage of clichés but are among the highest in their use of qualifiers, such as "very." He attributes those "verys" to fashions of literature in Austen's day. We might ask, too, how often Austen uses that sort of word with an ironic intent, in order to reveal a character's, or an idea's, being over the top. Sometimes in Austen, a "very" is just a "very." At others, it's offered with a wink and a nod.

Perhaps that complex mixture is an indication of how she would have reacted to a book of her own quotations, too. Her fiction demonstrates skepticism toward those who compile or consume snippets of words. That's only understandable. She crafted full-length novels of genius, in an age in which the bread-and-butter of book reviews was providing readers with exceptionally long extracts. These super-sized quotations—they might go on for pages—served to advertise complete novels. But they also allowed readers who didn't want to commit to an entire book to feign familiarity with an author and his or her work. Quoting from things, and keeping collections of quotations, was certainly trendy. Many educated people kept a personal commonplace book. In a blank volume, one might handwrite one's favorite epigrams. That activity echoed the print format of a then-ubiquitous book, Vicesimus Knox's *Elegant Extracts; or, Useful and Entertaining Passages in Prose* (1783). Its title clearly communicates the qualities it claimed to foster.

Austen didn't just poke fun at modish extract books but also at the opportunism and lack of originality of those who set out to create them. (This point is not lost on your fearless editor!) Such literary recyclers are ridiculed in Austen's now-famous defense of novels in *Northanger Abbey*. She scoffs at "the man who collects . . . some dozen lines of Milton, Pope, and Prior, with a paper from the Spectator" to publish them, implying that such volumes don't deserve applause (see November, p. 159). Quotation, misquotation, and mash-ups were a normal, and pleasurable, part of early nineteenth-century literary life. Austen, who loved wordplay of all kinds, wouldn't have rejected the entire mode. She was seemingly not against judicious quoting, verbally or in writing, because she engaged in the practice herself, often for comic effect. In a letter to her sister Cassandra, Jane once rewrote a line from Sir Walter Scott's poem *Marmion*, giving it her own meter and rhyme (see the entry for January 29). Austen's version is "I do not write for such dull Elves" / "As have not a great deal of Ingenuity themselves." It echoes and improves on Scott's original: "I do not rhyme to that dull elf, / Who cannot image to himself." So, for Austen, perhaps it's not the act of quotation that's the problem. Its value would seem to hinge on the who, what, how, and why of doing it.

In her fiction, the ways in which characters memorize, recite, and misquote are highly revealing. *Emma*'s valetudinarian innocent, Mr. Woodhouse, Emma's father, can't remember all of the lines of the bawdy limerick he was taught when young, try as he might. *Mansfield Park*'s Fanny Price is ridiculed by her cruel cousins, Maria and Julia Bertram, because she can't recite the names of English kings and Roman emperors, which they say makes them far cleverer than she is. (They're wrong.) *Pride and Prejudice*'s pedantic and conceited Mary Bennet enjoys trotting out bromides from the day's conduct books in tone-deaf, simplistic "moral extractions" (see the entries for August 7 and October 6). Nothing to admire there. But when *Emma*'s Mrs. Elton declares that she cannot quote any bits of prose or verse because "I am not one of those who have witty things at every body's service," we're surely not supposed to admire her for it.

All of this makes reading—and quoting from— Austen a surprisingly fraught enterprise. It's difficult to discern if any given line of her prose is laudable, laughable, or lamentable, much less when a very is only a very. The best example of just how complicated things have become in quoting Austen may be glimpsed in the line recently chosen by the Bank of England to accompany her face on the ten-pound note. The quoted line that sits just below Austen's portrait on the currency seems, at first glance, charmingly inoffensive: "I declare after all there is no enjoyment like reading" (see the entry for April 24). The problem is that this line is not in Austen's own voice. It's not even from the mouth of a likable character. It is spoken by *Pride and Prejudice*'s loathsome sham-reader, Caroline Bingley, who exhibits absolutely no enjoyment of reading. She yawns once before declaring this supposed enjoyment and once afterward. How could the Bank of England have gotten it so wrong? One suspects that someone went to BrainyQuote.com thinking, "Ooh! Let's find something smart Austen said about books or reading." Thanks to such websites, as well as those ubiquitous mugs and T-shirts, quoting ironic Austenian digs as if they are serious affirmations is incredibly tough to put a stop to. Such errors have a sad tendency to proliferate.

That's why Austen quotation books—even this one—ought to come with warning labels. It's absolutely delightful to read Austen in short bursts, whether you know her fiction well or not. Bits and pieces stand on their own as provocative, pleasing, or comic material. But to really grasp and appreciate the layers of meaning in her writing, you often need more than a single line. That's because her single lines are rarely *only* stand-alone witticisms. The exception to that is her letters, which are full of legitimate one-liners, delivering compact thoughts that pack a punch. My favorite is from an 1811 letter to her sister Cassandra. Jane tells her, "I will not say that your Mulberry trees are dead, but I am afraid they are not alive." No context is needed to appreciate the direct-indirection, communicated with equal parts sad seriousness and snark.

That's not usually the case in Austen. We can see that in another favored quotation, one that's often printed on pillows and framable artwork: "There is nothing like staying at home for real comfort." Celestial Seasonings used the line on its collectible tea packaging in the early 2000s, featuring a friendly looking bear in a light-blue nightshirt and red stocking cap. The bear sits in front of a fire, holding a cat on its lap, just below the words, "'Ah! There is nothing like staying at home for real comfort.'—Jane Austen." Again, the trouble is that although Austen *wrote* this line, she did not offer it up straight. It's delivered by *Emma*'s odious Mrs. Elton, a character who is always protesting too much and touting her own superiority over others. None of this is easily unraveled through snippet quotations.

What is clear is that this line doesn't just operate on a surface level. When Mrs. Elton recommends the comforts of home, she boastingly says, "Ah! there is nothing like staying at home, for real comfort. Nobody can be more devoted to home than I am. I was quite a proverb for it at Maple Grove" (see the entry for July 24). Two lines later, however, she's criticizing those who choose seclusion from the world. Then she backtracks on that sentiment, too, calling for the avoidance of either extreme in one's attachment to or detachment from home. Like much of what Mrs. Elton says, this line is self-satisfied and ridiculous. As readers, we're left wondering whether the touted comforts of home are supposed to be interpreted as an admirable sentiment out of the mouth of a flawed character, a false sentiment from a false one, or something else entirely. The reader must consider. What this certainly *is not* is a forthright piece of moralizing about the comforts of home.

Even worse is when words purporting to be Austen quotations turn out to be no such thing. Often, it's a movie quote masquerading as original Austen. Passed around in social-media memes and etched onto jewelry, these fake quotations circulate and recirculate. One of the greatest culprits is the line, "You have bewitched me, body and soul, and I love . . . I love . . . I love you!" This isn't vintage Austen. It's from director Joe Wright's *Pride and Prejudice* (2005), in a line lugubriously delivered by Matthew Macfadyen's Mr. Darcy to Keira Knightley's Elizabeth Bennet. Who needs such counterfeit Austen, when the real thing offers so many superior lines? Asked by Elizabeth when he first fell in love with her, Darcy replies, "I cannot fix on the hour, or the spot, or the look, or the words, which laid the foundation. It is too long ago. I was in the middle before I knew that I *had* begun" (see the entry for August 20).

You can begin reading this book on any page,

beginning, middle, or end. It contains 378 genuine, Austen-authored quotations. They're spread throughout the year, one a day, with longer selections chosen to begin each month. Most of these quotations first appeared in one of Austen's six major novels (*Sense and Sensibility* [1811], *Pride and Prejudice* [1813], *Mansfield Park* [1814], *Emma* [1816], *Northanger Abbey* [1818], and *Persuasion* [1818]), with further words drawn from her letters, of which only a paltry total of 161 survive. For those not well versed in things Austen, the most surprising quotations may be the ones from her raucous youthful writings, called *Juvenilia*; from *Lady Susan*, the early epistolary novel centered on a merry widow; and from the two fragment novels, *The Watsons* and *Sanditon*. If you don't know them, then the quotations in evidence here ought to propel you forward to read more and differently.

When a given quotation is in Austen's own voice (usually from her letters) or appears in the voice of a narrator, that's indicated by the title of the work being provided above the quotation. If the line or lines come from the mouths or thoughts of particular characters, that's clearly noted, too, in order for readers to carefully consider the source. Whenever possible, I've tried to provide the lines surrounding a pithy, oft-quoted sentence, to showcase it in its wider —even if only slightly wider!—context. Whether you approach this book on a one-a-day model, or in a satisfying binge read, you should emerge wiser about Austen, if not about life. Quoting her is the second-best recipe for happiness I've ever heard of.*

Your humble & obedient servant,

DEVONEY LOOSER

*See the entry for August 30.

THE DAILY JANE AUSTEN

JANUARY

It is a truth universally acknowledged, that a single man in possession of a good fortune, must be in want of a wife.

However little known the feelings or views of such a man may be on his first entering a neighbourhood, this truth is so well fixed in the minds of the surrounding families, that he is considered as the rightful property of some one or other of their daughters.

"My dear Mr. Bennet," said his lady to him one day, "have you heard that Netherfield Park is let at last?"

Mr. Bennet replied that he had not.

"But it is," returned she; "for Mrs. Long has just been here, and she told me all about it."

Mr. Bennet made no answer.

"Do you not want to know who has taken it?" cried his wife impatiently.

"*You* want to tell me, and I have no objection to hearing it."

This was invitation enough.

Pride and Prejudice (1813)

༺༻

JANUARY 1

NORTHANGER ABBEY (1818)

If adventures will not befal a young lady in her own village, she must seek them abroad.

JANUARY 2

MANSFIELD PARK (1814)

I purposely abstain from dates on this occasion, that every one may be at liberty to fix their own, aware that the cure of unconquerable passions, and the transfer of unchanging attachments, must vary much as to time in different people.

JANUARY 3

PERSUASION (1818)

How quick come the reasons for approving what we like!

"Well, it don't signify talking, but when a young man, be he who he will, comes and makes love to a pretty girl, and promises marriage, he has no business to fly off from his word only because he grows poor, and a richer girl is ready to have him. Why don't he, in such a case, sell his horses, let his house, turn off his servants, and make a thorough reform at once? I warrant you, Miss Marianne would have been ready to wait till matters came round. But that won't do, now-a-days; nothing in the way of pleasure can ever be given up by the young men of this age."

I am much obliged to you my dear Friend, for your advice respecting M^r. De Courcy . . . tho' I am not quite determined on following it.—I cannot easily resolve on anything so serious as Marriage, especially as I am not at present in want of money, & might perhaps till the old Gentleman's death, be very little benefited by the match. It is true that I am vain enough to beleive it within my reach.—I have made him sensible of my power, & can now enjoy the pleasure of triumphing over a Mind prepared to dislike me, & prejudiced against all my past actions.

JANUARY 6

EMMA (1816), EMMA WOODHOUSE
TO HARRIET SMITH

"I have none of the usual inducements of women to marry. Were I to fall in love, indeed, it would be a different thing! but I never have been in love; it is not my way, or my nature; and I do not think I ever shall. And, without love, I am sure I should be a fool to change such a situation as mine. Fortune I do not want; employment I do not want; consequence I do not want: I believe few married women are half as much mistress of their husband's house, as I am of Hartfield; and never, never could I expect to be so truly beloved and important; so always first and always right in any man's eyes as I am in my father's."

JANUARY 7

PRIDE AND PREJUDICE (1813),
ELIZABETH BENNET TO JANE BENNET

"What could be more natural than his asking you again? He could not help seeing that you were about five times as pretty as every other woman in the room. No thanks to his gallantry for that. Well, he certainly is very agreeable, and I give you leave to like him. You have liked many a stupider person."

JANUARY 8

NORTHANGER ABBEY (1818),
CATHERINE MORLAND TO ISABELLA THORPE

"Oh! yes, quite; what can it be?—But do not tell me—I would not be told upon any account. I know it must be a skeleton, I am sure it is Laurentina's skeleton. Oh! I am delighted with the book! I should like to spend my whole life in reading it. I assure you, if it had not been to meet you, I would not have come away from it for all the world."

JANUARY 9

THE BEAUTIFULL CASSANDRA (C. 1788)

Chapter the 3rd. The first person she met, was the Viscount of —— a young man, no less celebrated for his Accomplishments and Virtues, than for his Elegance and Beauty. She curtseyed and walked on. *Chapter the 4th.* She then proceeded to a Pastry-cooks where she devoured six ices, refused to pay for them, knocked down the Pastry Cook and walked away.

JANUARY 10

LETTER FROM JANE AUSTEN TO
CASSANDRA AUSTEN, 9–10 JANUARY 1796

I am almost afraid to tell you how my Irish friend
and I behaved. Imagine to yourself everything most
profligate and shocking in the way of dancing and
sitting down together.

JANUARY 11

LADY SUSAN (C. 1794–1805),
MRS. JOHNSON TO LADY SUSAN VERNON

She arrived yesterday in pursuit of her Husband;—
but perhaps you know this already from himself.—
She came to this house to entreat my Husband's
interference, & before I could be aware of it, everything that you could wish to be concealed, was
known to him; & unluckily she had wormed out of
Manwaring's servant that he had visited you every
day since your being in Town, & had just watched
him to your door herself!—What could I do?—Facts
are such horrid things!

At last he turned round again, and regarded them both; she started up, and pronouncing his name in a tone of affection, held out her hand to him. He approached, and addressing himself rather to Elinor than Marianne, as if wishing to avoid her eye, and determined not to observe her attitude, inquired in a hurried manner after Mrs. Dashwood, and asked how long they had been in town. Elinor was robbed of all presence of mind by such an address, and was unable to say a word. But the feelings of her sister were instantly expressed. Her face was crimsoned over, and she exclaimed in a voice of the greatest emotion, "Good God! Willoughby, what is the meaning of this? Have you not received my letters? Will you not shake hands with me?"

"When an old lady plays the fool, it is not in the course of nature that she should suffer from it many years."

I am very much flattered by your commendation of my last Letter, for I write only for Fame, and without any view to pecuniary Emolument.

JANUARY 15

PRIDE AND PREJUDICE (1813),
CHARLOTTE LUCAS AND ELIZABETH BENNET

"Happiness in marriage is entirely a matter of chance. If the dispositions of the parties are ever so well known to each other, or ever so similar beforehand, it does not advance their felicity in the least. They always contrive to grow sufficiently unlike afterwards to have their share of vexation; and it is better to know as little as possible of the defects of the person with whom you are to pass your life."

"You make me laugh, Charlotte; but it is not sound. You know it is not sound, and that you would never act in this way yourself."

"But indeed I cannot go. If I am wrong, I am doing what I believe to be right."

JANUARY 17

"Aye my dear—that's very sensibly said," cried Lady Denham. "And if we could but get a young heiress to Sanditon! But heiresses are monstrous scarce! I do not think we have had an heiress here, or even a co, since Sanditon has been a public place. Families come after families, but as far as I can learn, it is not one in an hundred of them that have any real property, landed or funded.—An income perhaps, but no property. Clergymen may be, or lawyers from town, or half pay officers, or widows with only a jointure. And what good can such people do anybody?—except just as they take our empty houses—and (between ourselves) I think they are great fools for not staying at home. Now, if we could get a young heiress to be sent here for her health—(and if she was ordered to drink asses' milk I could supply her)—and as soon as she got well, have her fall in love with Sir Edward!"

JANUARY 18

No one who had ever seen Catherine Morland in her infancy, would have supposed her born to be an heroine. Her situation in life, the character of her father and mother, her own person and disposition, were all equally against her. Her father was a clergyman, without being neglected, or poor, and a very respectable man, though his name was Richard—and he had never been handsome. He had a considerable independence besides two good livings—and he was not in the least addicted to locking up his daughters. Her mother was a woman of useful plain sense, with a good temper, and, what is more remarkable, with a good constitution. She had three sons before Catherine was born; and instead of dying in bringing the latter into the world, as any body might expect, she still lived on—lived to have six children more—to see them growing up around her, and to enjoy excellent health herself.

JANUARY 19

Perfect happiness, even in memory, is not common.

JANUARY 20

Sir Edward's great object in life was to be seductive.
—With such personal advantages as he knew himself to possess, and such talents as he did also give
himself credit for, he regarded it as his duty.—He
felt that he was formed to be a dangerous man.

JANUARY 21

Clara saw through him, and had not the least inten-
tion of being seduced.

JANUARY 22

[Catherine Morland] had reached the age of seventeen, without having seen one amiable youth who
could call forth her sensibility; without having in-
spired one real passion, and without having excited
even any admiration but what was very moderate
and very transient. This was strange indeed! But
strange things may be generally accounted for if
their cause be fairly searched out. There was not one

lord in the neighbourhood; no—not even a baronet. There was not one family among their acquaintance who had reared and supported a boy accidentally found at their door—not one young man whose origin was unknown. Her father had no ward, and the squire of the parish no children.

But when a young lady is to be a heroine, the perverseness of forty surrounding families cannot prevent her. Something must and will happen to throw a hero in her way.

JANUARY 23

LETTER FROM JANE AUSTEN TO
CASSANDRA AUSTEN, 21–23 JANUARY 1799

I do not think it worth while to wait for enjoyment until there is some real opportunity for it.

JANUARY 24

LETTER FROM JANE AUSTEN TO
CASSANDRA AUSTEN, 24 JANUARY 1813

Mr Digweed has used us basely. Handsome is as Handsome does; he is therefore a very ill-looking Man.

"But that expression of 'violently in love' is so hackneyed, so doubtful, so indefinite, that it gives me very little idea. It is as often applied to feelings which arise only from an half hour's acquaintance, as to a real, strong attachment. Pray, how *violent was* Mr. Bingley's love?"

"I never saw a more promising inclination. He was growing quite inattentive to other people, and wholly engrossed by her. Every time they met, it was more decided and remarkable. At his own ball he offended two or three young ladies, by not asking them to dance, and I spoke to him twice myself, without receiving an answer. Could there be finer symptoms? Is not general incivility the very essence of love?"

"Oh! I always deserve the best treatment, because I never put up with any other."

JANUARY 27

"I do assure you, Sir, that I have no pretension whatever to that kind of elegance which consists in tormenting a respectable man. I would rather be paid the compliment of being believed sincere. I thank you again and again for the honour you have done me in your proposals, but to accept them is absolutely impossible. My feelings in every respect forbid it. Can I speak plainer? Do not consider me now as an elegant female intending to plague you, but as a rational creature speaking the truth from her heart."

"You are uniformly charming!" cried he, with an air of awkward gallantry; "and I am persuaded that when sanctioned by the express authority of both your excellent parents, my proposals will not fail of being acceptable."

To such perseverance in wilful self-deception Elizabeth would make no reply.

JANUARY 28

"I never spent a pleasanter morning in my life."

"I am afraid," replied Elinor, "that the pleasantness of an employment does not always evince its propriety."

"On the contrary, nothing can be a stronger proof of it, Elinor; for if there had been any real impropriety in what I did, I should have been sensible of it at the time, for we always know when we are acting wrong, and with such a conviction I could have had no pleasure."

"But, my dear Marianne, as it has already exposed you to some very impertinent remarks, do you not now begin to doubt the discretion of your own conduct?"

"If the impertinent remarks of Mrs. Jennings are to be the proof of impropriety in conduct, we are all offending every moment of all our lives. I value not her censure any more than I should do her commendation."

JANUARY 29

LETTER FROM JANE AUSTEN TO
CASSANDRA AUSTEN, 29 JANUARY 1813

I must confess that *I* think [Elizabeth Bennet] as delightful a creature as ever appeared in print, & how I shall be able to tolerate those who do not like *her* at least, I do not know.—There are a few Typical errors—& a "said he" or a "said she" would sometimes make the Dialogue more immediately clear—but "I do not write for such dull Elves" / "As have not a great deal of Ingenuity themselves."

"Westgate-buildings!" said he; "and who is Miss Anne Elliot to be visiting in Westgate-buildings?—A Mrs. Smith. A widow Mrs. Smith,—and who was her husband? One of the five thousand Mr. Smiths whose names are to be met with every where. And what is her attraction? That she is old and sickly.—Upon my word, Miss Anne Elliot, you have the most extraordinary taste! Every thing that revolts other people, low company, paltry rooms, foul air, disgusting associations are inviting to you. But surely, you may put off this old lady till to-morrow. She is not so near her end, I presume, but that she may hope to see another day. What is her age? Forty?"

JANUARY 31

MANSFIELD PARK (1814), MARY CRAWFORD
AND FANNY PRICE, ON HENRY CRAWFORD

"Ah! I cannot deny it. He has now and then been a sad flirt, and cared very little for the havock he might be making in young ladies' affections. I have often scolded him for it, but it is his only fault; and there is this to be said, that very few young ladies have any affections worth caring for. And then, Fanny, the glory of fixing one who has been shot at by so many; of having it in one's power to pay off the debts of one's sex! Oh, I am sure it is not in woman's nature to refuse such a triumph."

Fanny shook her head. "I cannot think well of a man who sports with any woman's feelings; and there may often be a great deal more suffered than a stander-by can judge of."

FEBRUARY

"Your sister, I understand, does not approve of second attachments."

"No," replied Elinor, "her opinions are all romantic."

"Or rather, as I believe, she considers them impossible to exist."

"I believe she does. But how she contrives it without reflecting on the character of her own father, who had himself two wives, I know not. A few years however will settle her opinions on the reasonable basis of common sense and observation; and then they may be more easy to define and to justify than they now are, by any body but herself."

"This will probably be the case," he replied; "and yet there is something so amiable in the prejudices of a young mind, that one is sorry to see them give way to the reception of more general opinions."

"I cannot agree with you there," said Elinor. "There are inconveniences attending such feelings as Marianne's, which all the charms of enthusiasm and ignorance of the world cannot atone for. Her systems have all the unfortunate tendency of setting propriety at nought; and a better acquaintance with the world is what I look forward to as her greatest possible advantage."

Sense and Sensibility (1811),
Colonel Brandon and Elinor Dashwood

FEBRUARY 1

SANDITON (1817)

Miss Lambe was beyond comparison the most important and precious, as she paid in proportion to her fortune.—She was about seventeen, half mulatto, chilly and tender, had a maid of her own, was to have the best room in the lodgings, and was always of the first consequence in every plan.

FEBRUARY 2

MANSFIELD PARK (1814)

To the education of her daughters, Lady Bertram paid not the smallest attention. She had not time for such cares. She was a woman who spent her days in sitting nicely dressed on a sofa, doing some long piece of needle-work, of little use and no beauty, thinking more of her pug than her children, but very indulgent to the latter, when it did not put herself to inconvenience, guided in every thing important by Sir Thomas, and in smaller concerns by her sister. Had she possessed greater leisure for the service of her girls, she would probably have supposed it unnecessary, for they were under the care of a governess, with proper masters, and could want nothing more. As for Fanny's being stupid at learning, "she could only say it was very unlucky, but some people *were* stupid, and Fanny must take more pains; she did not know what else was to be done; and except her being so dull, she must add, she saw no harm in the poor little thing—and always found her very handy and quick in carrying messages, and fetching what she wanted."

FEBRUARY 3

PRIDE AND PREJUDICE (1813),
MR. DARCY AND ELIZABETH BENNET

"My good opinion once lost is lost forever."

"*That* is a failing indeed!"—cried Elizabeth. "Implacable resentment *is* a shade in a character. But you have chosen your fault well.—I really cannot *laugh* at it. You are safe from me."

"There is, I believe, in every disposition a tendency to some particular evil, a natural defect, which not even the best education can overcome."

"And *your* defect is a propensity to hate every body."

"And yours," he replied with a smile, "is wilfully to misunderstand them."

FEBRUARY 4

SENSE AND SENSIBILITY (1811),
ELINOR DASHWOOD TO MR. WILLOUGHBY

"Well, sir—be quick—and if you can—less violent."

FEBRUARY 5

"I was proud, too proud to ask again. I did not understand you. I shut my eyes, and would not understand you, or do you justice. This is a recollection which ought to make me forgive every one sooner than myself. Six years of separation and suffering might have been spared. It is a sort of pain, too, which is new to me. I have been used to the gratification of believing myself to earn every blessing that I enjoyed. I have valued myself on honourable toils and just rewards. Like other great men under reverses," he added with a smile. "I must endeavour to subdue my mind to my fortune. I must learn to brook being happier than I deserve."

FEBRUARY 6

"Mama, the more I know of the world, the more I am convinced that I shall never see a man whom I can really love. I require so much!"

FEBRUARY 7

"Time will generally lessen the interest of every attachment not within the daily circle."

FEBRUARY 8

"Lovely and too charming Fair one, notwithstanding your forbidding Squint, your greazy tresses and your swelling Back, which are more frightfull than imagination can paint or pen describe, I cannot refrain from expressing my raptures, at the engaging Qualities of your Mind, which so amply atone for the Horror, with which your first appearance must ever inspire the unwary visitor."

FEBRUARY 9

"His fault, the liking to make girls a little in love with him, is not half so dangerous to a wife's happiness, as a tendency to fall in love himself, which he has never been addicted to."

FEBRUARY 10

SANDITON (1817),
CHARLOTTE HEYWOOD'S THOUGHTS

Charlotte could not but think of the extreme difficulty which secret lovers must have in finding a proper spot for their stolen interviews.

FEBRUARY 11

SENSE AND SENSIBILITY (1811),
FANNY DASHWOOD TO MR. JOHN DASHWOOD, ON
HIS STEPMOTHER, MRS. DASHWOOD

"People always live for ever when there is any annuity to be paid them; and she is very stout and healthy, and hardly forty. An annuity is a very serious business; it comes over and over every year, and there is no getting rid of it. You are not aware of what you are doing. I have known a great deal of the trouble of annuities; for my mother was clogged with the payment of three to old superannuated servants by my father's will, and it is amazing how disagreeable she found it. Twice every year these annuities were to be paid; and then there was the trouble of getting it to them; and then one of them was said to have died, and afterwards it turned out to be no such thing. My mother was quite sick of it."

FEBRUARY 12

PERSUASION (1818)

Vanity was the beginning and the end of Sir Walter Elliot's character; vanity of person and of situation. He had been remarkably handsome in his youth; and, at fifty-four, was still a very fine man. Few women could think more of their personal appearance than he did; nor could the valet of any new made lord be more delighted with the place he held in society. He considered the blessing of beauty as inferior only to the blessing of a baronetcy; and the Sir Walter Elliot, who united these gifts, was the constant object of his warmest respect and devotion.

FEBRUARY 13

LADY SUSAN (C. 1794–1805),
LADY SUSAN VERNON TO MRS. JOHNSON, ON
HER BROTHER-IN-LAW, CHARLES VERNON

I really have a regard for him, he is so easily imposed on!

FEBRUARY 14

SENSE AND SENSIBILITY (1811)

Though a very few hours spent in the hard labour of incessant talking will dispatch more subjects than can really be in common between any two rational creatures, yet with lovers it is different. Between *them* no subject is finished, no communication is even made, till it has been made at least twenty times over.

FEBRUARY 15

NORTHANGER ABBEY (1818)

Catherine was delighted with this extension of her Bath acquaintance, and almost forgot Mr. Tilney while she talked to Miss Thorpe. Friendship is certainly the finest balm for the pangs of disappointed love.

FEBRUARY 16

PRIDE AND PREJUDICE (1813),
MR. DARCY TO CAROLINE BINGLEY

"A lady's imagination is very rapid; it jumps from admiration to love, from love to matrimony in a moment."

FEBRUARY 17

"How wonderful, how very wonderful the operations of time, and the changes of the human mind!"

FEBRUARY 18

"A woman in love with one man cannot flirt with another."

"It is probable that she will neither love so well, nor flirt so well, as she might do either singly."

FEBRUARY 19

I have more than once repented that I did not marry him myself, & were he but one degree less contemptibly weak I certainly should, but I must own myself rather romantic in that respect, & that Riches only, will not satisfy me.

FEBRUARY 20

MANSFIELD PARK (1814), EDMUND BERTRAM
TO MARY CRAWFORD AND FANNY PRICE

"We do not look in great cities for our best morality."

FEBRUARY 21

PERSUASION (1818), ANNE ELLIOT'S THOUGHTS

She distrusted the past, if not the present.

FEBRUARY 22

PRIDE AND PREJUDICE (1813),
ELIZABETH BENNET TO MR. DARCY

"You are mistaken, Mr. Darcy, if you suppose that the mode of your declaration affected me in any other way, than as it spared me the concern which I might have felt in refusing you, had you behaved in a more gentleman-like manner."

She saw him start at this, but he said nothing, and she continued,

"You could not have made me the offer of your hand in any possible way that would have tempted me to accept it."

Again his astonishment was obvious; and he

looked at her with an expression of mingled incredulity and mortification.

FEBRUARY 23

LADY SUSAN (C. 1794–1805),
CATHERINE VERNON TO LADY DE COURCY

There are plenty of books in the room, but it is not every girl who has been running wild the first fifteen years of her life, that can or will read.

FEBRUARY 24

SENSE AND SENSIBILITY (1811)

Marianne was still handsomer. Her form, though not so correct as her sister's, in having the advantage of height, was more striking; and her face was so lovely, that when in the common cant of praise she was called a beautiful girl, truth was less violently outraged than usually happens.

FEBRUARY 25

"I am very strong. Nothing ever fatigues me, but doing what I do not like."

FEBRUARY 26

Miss F. —Pray be seated.

(They sit)

Bless me! there ought to be 8 Chairs and these are but 6. However, if your Ladyship will but take Sir Arthur in your Lap, and Sophy, my Brother in hers, I beleive we shall do pretty well.

FEBRUARY 27

"I still think you see things too strongly; and I really cannot undertake to harangue all the rest upon a subject of this kind.—*There* would be the greatest indecorum I think."

"Do you imagine that I could have such an idea

in my head? No—let your conduct be the only harangue."

FEBRUARY 28

SENSE AND SENSIBILITY (1811)

[John Dashwood] was not an ill-disposed young man, unless to be rather cold hearted, and rather selfish, is to be ill-disposed: but he was, in general, well respected; for he conducted himself with propriety in the discharge of his ordinary duties. Had he married a more amiable woman, he might have been made still more respectable than he was:—he might even have been made amiable himself; for he was very young when he married, and very fond of his wife. But Mrs. John Dashwood was a strong caricature of himself;—more narrow-minded and selfish.

FEBRUARY 29

MANSFIELD PARK (1814), MARY CRAWFORD
TO EDMUND BERTRAM

"Oh! do not attack me with your watch. A watch is always too fast or too slow. I cannot be dictated to by a watch."

MARCH

"I can listen no longer in silence. I must speak to you by such means as are within my reach. You pierce my soul. I am half agony, half hope. Tell me not that I am too late, that such precious feelings are gone for ever. I offer myself to you again with a heart even more your own, than when you almost broke it eight years and a half ago. Dare not say that man forgets sooner than woman, that his love has an earlier death. I have loved none but you. Unjust I may have been, weak and resentful I have been, but never inconstant. You alone have brought me to Bath. For you alone I think and plan.—Have you not seen this? Can you fail to have understood my wishes?—I had not waited even these ten days, could I have read your feelings, as I think you must have penetrated mine. I can hardly write. I am every instant hearing something which overpowers me. You sink your voice, but I can distinguish the tones of that voice, when they would be lost on others.— Too good, too excellent creature! You do us justice indeed. You do believe that there is true attachment and constancy among men. Believe it to be most fervent, most undeviating in

F. W.

"I must go, uncertain of my fate; but I shall return hither, or follow your party, as soon as possible. A word, a look will be enough to decide whether I enter your father's house this evening, or never."

Persuasion (1818),
Captain Wentworth writing to Anne Elliot

"That is an expression, Sir John," said Marianne, warmly, "which I particularly dislike. I abhor every common-place phrase by which wit is intended; and 'setting one's cap at a man,' or 'making a conquest,' are the most odious of all. Their tendency is gross and illiberal; and if their construction could ever be deemed clever, time has long ago destroyed all its ingenuity."

"Emma is spoiled by being the cleverest of her family. At ten years old, she had the misfortune of being able to answer questions which puzzled her sister at seventeen. She was always quick and assured: Isabella slow and diffident. And ever since she was twelve, Emma has been mistress of the house and of you all. In her mother she lost the only person able to cope with her."

MARCH 3

SENSE AND SENSIBILITY (1811)

Though nothing could be more polite than Lady Middleton's behaviour to Elinor and Marianne, she did not really like them at all. Because they neither flattered herself nor her children, she could not believe them good-natured; and because they were fond of reading, she fancied them satirical: perhaps without exactly knowing what it was to be satirical; but *that* did not signify. It was censure in common use, and easily given.

MARCH 4

SANDITON (1817), MR. TOM PARKER TO CHARLOTTE HEYWOOD, ON HIS BROTHER SIDNEY PARKER

"Sidney says any thing you know. He has always said what he chose of and to us all. Most families have such a member among them I believe Miss Heywood.—There is a someone in most families privileged by superior abilities or spirits to say anything.—In ours, it is Sidney; who is a very clever young man, and with great powers of pleasing.—He lives too much in the world to be settled; that is his only fault.—He is here and there and every where."

"But think no more of the letter. The feelings of the person who wrote, and the person who received it, are now so widely different from what they were then, that every unpleasant circumstance attending it, ought to be forgotten. You must learn some of my philosophy. Think only of the past as its remembrance gives you pleasure."

[Catherine Morland] went home very happy. The morning had answered all her hopes, and the evening of the following day was now the object of expectation, the future good. What gown and what head-dress she should wear on the occasion became her chief concern. She cannot be justified in it. Dress is at all times a frivolous distinction, and excessive solicitude about it often destroys its own aim. Catherine knew all this very well; her great aunt had read her a lecture on the subject only the Christmas before; and yet she lay awake ten minutes on Wednesday night debating between her spotted and her tamboured muslin, and nothing but the shortness of the time prevented her buying a new one for the evening.

MARCH 7

SENSE AND SENSIBILITY (1811)

But [Edward Ferrars] was neither fitted by abilities nor disposition to answer the wishes of his mother and sister, who longed to see him distinguished— as—they hardly knew what. They wanted him to make a fine figure in the world in some manner or other. His mother wished to interest him in political concerns, to get him into parliament, or to see him connected with some of the great men of the day. Mrs. John Dashwood wished it likewise; but in the mean while, till one of these superior blessings could be attained, it would have quieted her ambition to see him driving a barouche. But Edward had no turn for great men or barouches. All his wishes centered in domestic comfort and the quiet of private life. Fortunately he had a younger brother who was more promising.

MARCH 8

SANDITON (1817)

Beauty, sweetness, poverty and dependance, do not want the imagination of a man to operate upon.

With due exceptions—woman feels for woman very promptly and compassionately.

MARCH 9

MANSFIELD PARK (1814)

With so much true merit and true love, and no want of fortune or friends, the happiness of the married cousins must appear as secure as earthly happiness can be.—Equally formed for domestic life, and attached to country pleasures, their home was the home of affection and comfort.

MARCH 10

NORTHANGER ABBEY (1818)
CATHERINE MORLAND AND HENRY TILNEY

"I am sure," cried Catherine, "I did not mean to say any thing wrong; but it *is* a nice book, and why should not I call it so?"

"Very true," said Henry, "and this is a very nice day, and we are taking a very nice walk, and you are two very nice young ladies. Oh! it is a very nice word indeed!—it does for every thing."

MARCH 11

She acknowledged it to be very fitting, that every little social commonwealth should dictate its own matters of discourse.

MARCH 12

She doubted whether she had not transgressed the duty of woman by woman.

MARCH 13

Single Women have a dreadful propensity for being poor—which is one very strong argument in favour of Matrimony, but I need not dwell on such arguments with *you*, pretty Dear, you do not want inclination.—Well, I shall say, as I have often said before, Donot be in a hurry; depend upon it, the right Man will come at last; you will in the course of the next two or three years, meet with somebody more generally unexceptionable than anyone you have yet known, who will love you as warmly as ever

He did, & who will so completely attach you, that you will feel you never really loved before.

PERSUASION (1818), MRS. SMITH TO ANNE ELLIOT

"There is so little real friendship in the world!"

SENSE AND SENSIBILITY (1811), MARIANNE
DASHWOOD TO ELINOR DASHWOOD

Her heart was hardened against the belief of Mrs. Jennings's entering into her sorrows with any compassion.

"No, no, no, it cannot be," she cried; "she cannot feel. Her kindness is not sympathy; her good nature is not tenderness. All that she wants is gossip, and she only likes me now because I supply it."

Elinor had not needed this to be assured of the injustice to which her sister was often led in her opinion of others, by the irritable refinement of her own mind, and the too great importance placed by her on the delicacies of a strong sensibility, and the graces of a polished manner. Like half the rest of the world, if more than half there be that are clever and good, Marianne, with excellent abilities and an excellent disposition, was neither reasonable nor candid. She expected from other people the same opinions and feelings as her own, and she judged of their motives by the immediate effect of their actions on herself.

MARCH 16

MANSFIELD PARK (1814)

But Miss Frances married, in the common phrase, to disoblige her family, and by fixing on a Lieutenant of Marines, without education, fortune, or connections, did it very thoroughly. She could hardly have made a more untoward choice.

MARCH 17

SANDITON (1817), LADY DENHAM TO CHARLOTTE HEYWOOD, MR. TOM PARKER, AND OTHERS

"I am not a woman of parade, as all the world knows."

MARCH 18

He seemed very sentimental, very full of some feelings or other, and very much addicted to all the newest-fashioned hard words.

MARCH 19

"I am glad you approve of what I have done," said he very comfortably. "But I thought you would. Such schemes as these are nothing without numbers. One cannot have too large a party. A large party secures its own amusement. And [Mrs. Elton] is a good-natured woman after all. One could not leave her out."

MARCH 20

"The sooner every party breaks up, the better."

MARCH 21

THE WATSONS (C. 1803–5), ON EMMA WATSON

Many were the eyes, and various the degrees of approbation with which she was examined. Some saw no fault, and some no beauty—. With some her brown skin was the annihilation of every grace.

MARCH 22

PRIDE AND PREJUDICE (1813),
ELIZABETH BENNET AND MR. DARCY

"I wonder who first discovered the efficacy of poetry in driving away love!"

"I have been used to consider poetry as the *food* of love," said Darcy.

"Of a fine, stout, healthy love it may. Every thing nourishes what is strong already. But if it be only a slight, thin sort of inclination, I am convinced that one good sonnet will starve it entirely away."

MARCH 23

LETTER FROM JANE AUSTEN
TO FANNY KNIGHT, 23–25 MARCH 1817

He & I should not in the least agree of course, in our ideas of Novels & Heroines;—pictures of perfection as you know make me sick & wicked—but there is some very good sense in what he says, & I particularly respect him for wishing to think well of all young Ladies; it shews an amiable & a delicate Mind. —And he deserves better treatment than to be obliged to read any more of my Works.

MARCH 24

LOVE AND FREINDSHIP (C. 1790),
LAURA WRITING TO MARIANNE, QUOTING
MARIANNE'S MOTHER, ISABEL

"Beware my Laura (she would often say) Beware of the insipid Vanities and idle Dissipations of the Metropolis of England; Beware of the unmeaning Luxuries of Bath and of the Stinking fish of Southampton."

MARCH 25

PERSUASION (1818), SIR WALTER ELLIOT

He had frequently observed, as he walked, that one handsome face would be followed by thirty, or five and thirty frights; and once, as he had stood in a shop in Bond-street, he had counted eighty-seven women go by, one after another, without there being a tolerable face among them.

"With all due respect to such of the present company as chance to be married, my dear Mrs. Grant, there is not one in a hundred of either sex, who is not taken in when they marry. Look where I will, I see that it *is* so; and I feel that it *must* be so, when I consider that it is, of all transactions, the one in which people expect most from others, and are least honest themselves."

"We all like a play."

"What are Mrs. Ferrars's views for you at present, Edward?" said she, when dinner was over and they had drawn round the fire; "are you still to be a great orator in spite of yourself?"

"No. I hope my mother is now convinced that I have no more talents than inclination for a public life!"

"But how is your fame to be established? for famous you must be to satisfy all your family; and with no inclination for expense, no affection for strangers, no profession, and no assurance, you may find it a difficult matter."

"I shall not attempt it. I have no wish to be distinguished; and I have every reason to hope I never shall. Thank Heaven! I cannot be forced into genius and eloquence."

"You have no ambition, I well know. Your wishes are all moderate."

"As moderate as those of the rest of the world, I believe. I wish as well as every body else to be perfectly happy; but like every body else it must be in my own way. Greatness will not make me so."

MARCH 29

EMMA (1816), FRANK CHURCHILL
TO EMMA WOODHOUSE

"I am the wretchedest being in the world at a civil falsehood."

MARCH 30

"I am persuaded that you can be as insincere as your neighbours, when it is necessary."

MARCH 31

"I have no notion of treating men with such respect. *That* is the way to spoil them."

APRIL

"I remember hearing you once say, Mr. Darcy, that you hardly ever forgave, that your resentment once created was unappeasable. You are very cautious, I suppose, as to its *being created*."

"I am," said he, with a firm voice.

"And never allow yourself to be blinded by prejudice?"

"I hope not."

"It is particularly incumbent on those who never change their opinion, to be secure of judging properly at first."

"May I ask to what these questions tend?"

"Merely to the illustration of *your* character," said she, endeavouring to shake off her gravity. "I am trying to make it out."

"And what is your success?"

She shook her head. "I do not get on at all. I hear such different accounts of you as puzzle me exceedingly."

Pride and Prejudice (1813),
Elizabeth Bennet and Mr. Darcy

APRIL 1

LETTER FROM JANE AUSTEN TO
JAMES STANIER CLARKE, 1 APRIL 1816

I could not sit seriously down to write a serious Romance under any other motive than to save my Life, & if it were indispensable for me to keep it up & never relax into laughing at myself or other people, I am sure I should be hung before I had finished the first Chapter.

APRIL 2

EMMA (1816)

Every body was either surprized or not surprized.

APRIL 3

PERSUASION (1818)

He had, in fact, though his sisters were now doing all they could for him, by calling him "poor Richard," been nothing better than a thick-headed, unfeeling, unprofitable Dick Musgrove, who had never done any thing to entitle himself to more than the abbreviation of his name, living or dead.

APRIL 4

PRIDE AND PREJUDICE (1813)

[Mr. Bingley] was quite young, wonderfully handsome, extremely agreeable, and to crown the whole, he meant to be at the next assembly with a large party. Nothing could be more delightful! To be fond of dancing was a certain step towards falling in love; and very lively hopes of Mr. Bingley's heart were entertained.

APRIL 5

EMMA (1816)

Emma denied none of it aloud, and agreed to none of it in private.

APRIL 6

NORTHANGER ABBEY (1818), HENRY TILNEY
TO CATHERINE MORLAND

"If I understand you rightly, you had formed a surmise of such horror as I have hardly words to—Dear Miss Morland, consider the dreadful nature of the suspicions you have entertained. What have you been judging from? Remember the country and the age in which we live. Remember that we are English, that we are Christians. Consult your own understanding, your own sense of the probable, your own observation of what is passing around you—Does our education prepare us for such atrocities? Do our laws connive at them? Could they be perpetrated without being known, in a country like this, where social and literary intercourse is on such a footing; where every man is surrounded by a neighbourhood of voluntary spies, and where roads and newspapers lay every thing open? Dearest Miss Morland, what ideas have you been admitting?"

They had reached the end of the gallery; and with tears of shame she ran off to her own room.

"And yet I have heard that there is a great deal of wine drank in Oxford."

"Oxford! There is no drinking at Oxford now, I assure you. Nobody drinks there. You would hardly meet with a man who goes beyond his four pints at the utmost."

APRIL 8

"Vanity working on a weak head, produces every sort of mischief."

APRIL 9

"I certainly will not persuade myself to feel more than I do. I am quite enough in love. I should be sorry to be more."

APRIL 10

This violent oppression of spirits continued the whole evening. She was without any power, because she was without any desire of command over herself. The slightest mention of any thing relative to Willoughby overpowered her in an instant; and though her family were most anxiously attentive to her comfort, it was impossible for them, if they spoke at all, to keep clear of every subject which her feelings connected with him.

APRIL 11

An artist cannot do anything slovenly.

APRIL 12

MANSFIELD PARK (1814),
FANNY PRICE TO MR. RUSHWORTH

"When people are waiting, they are bad judges of time, and every half minute seems like five."

APRIL 13

FREDERIC AND ELFRIDA (C. 1787)

Mrs Fitzroy did not approve of the match on account of the tender years of the young couple, Rebecca being but 36 and Captain Roger little more than 63. To remedy this objection, it was agreed that they should wait a little while till they were a good deal older.

APRIL 14

"I am not fond of the idea of my shrubberies being always approachable."

APRIL 15

"We know how difficult it is to keep the actions and designs of one part of the world from the notice and curiosity of the other,—consequence has its tax."

APRIL 16

"Every body has their level: but as for myself, I am not, I think, quite so much at a loss. I need not so totally despair of an equal alliance, as to be addressing myself to Miss Smith!"

APRIL 17

"Run mad as often as you chuse; but do not faint—".

APRIL 18

I am sorry to tell you that I am getting very extravagant & spending all my Money; & what is worse for *you*, I have been spending yours too.

APRIL 19

"Oh!" cried Anne eagerly, "I hope I do justice to all that is felt by you, and by those who resemble you. God forbid that I should undervalue the warm and faithful feelings of any of my fellow-creatures. I should deserve utter contempt if I dared to suppose that true attachment and constancy were known only by woman. No, I believe you capable of every thing great and good in your married lives. I believe you equal to every important exertion, and

to every domestic forbearance, so long as—if I may
be allowed the expression, so long as you have an
object. I mean, while the woman you love lives, and
lives for you. All the privilege I claim for my own sex
(it is not a very enviable one, you need not covet it)
is that of loving longest, when existence or when
hope is gone."

APRIL 20

EMMA (1816), EMMA WOODHOUSE
AND FRANK CHURCHILL

Emma would not agree to this, and began a warm
defence of Miss Fairfax's complexion. "It was certainly never brilliant, but she would not allow it to
have a sickly hue in general; and there was a soft-
ness and delicacy in her skin which gave peculiar elegance to the character of her face." He listened with
all due deference; acknowledged that he had heard
many people say the same—but yet he must confess, that to him nothing could make amends for
the want of the fine glow of health. Where features
were indifferent, a fine complexion gave beauty
to them all; and where they were good, the effect
was—fortunately he need not attempt to describe
what the effect was.

"Well," said Emma, "there is no disputing about
taste.—At least you admire her except her complexion."

He shook his head and laughed.—"I cannot separate Miss Fairfax and her complexion."

APRIL 21

"And then when you go away! you may leave one or two of my sisters behind you; and I dare say I shall get husbands for them before the winter is over."

"I thank you for my share of the favour," said Elizabeth; "but I do not particularly like your way of getting husbands."

APRIL 22

"We are not all born to be handsome."

APRIL 23

"No doubt, one is familiar with Shakespeare in a degree," said Edmund, "from one's earliest years. His celebrated passages are quoted by every body; they are in half the books we open, and we all talk Shakespeare, use his similies, and describe with his descriptions; but this is totally distinct from giving his sense as you gave it. To know him in bits and scraps, is common enough; to know him pretty thoroughly, is, perhaps, not uncommon; but to read him well aloud, is no everyday talent."

APRIL 24

PRIDE AND PREJUDICE (1813), CAROLINE
BINGLEY TO MR. DARCY AND OTHERS

At length, quite exhausted by the attempt to be amused with her own book, which she had only chosen because it was the second volume of his, she gave a great yawn and said, "How pleasant it is to spend an evening in this way! I declare after all there is no enjoyment like reading! How much sooner one tires of any thing than of a book!—When I have a house of my own, I shall be miserable if I have not an excellent library."

No one made any reply. She then yawned again, threw aside her book, and cast her eyes round the room in quest of some amusement.

APRIL 25

He reasoned and talked in vain; she smiled and said, "I am determined I will:" he put out his hands; she was too precipitate by half a second, she fell on the pavement on the Lower Cobb, and was taken up lifeless!

There was no wound, no blood, no visible bruise; but her eyes were closed, she breathed not, her face was like death.—The horror of that moment to all who stood around!

APRIL 26

Anne wondered whether it ever occurred to him now, to question the justness of his own previous opinion as to the universal felicity and advantage of firmness of character; and whether it might not strike him, that, like all other qualities of the mind, it should have its proportions and limits. She thought it could scarcely escape him to feel, that a persuadable temper might sometimes be as much in favour of happiness, as a very resolute character.

"My illness, I well knew, had been entirely brought on by myself by such negligence of my own health, as I had felt even at the time to be wrong. Had I died,—it would have been self-destruction. I did not know my danger till the danger was removed; but with such feelings as these reflections gave me, I wonder at my recovery,—wonder that the very eagerness of my desire to live, to have time for atonement to my God, and to you all, did not kill me at once. Had I died,—in what peculiar misery should I have left you, my nurse, my friend, my sister!—You, who had seen all the fretful selfishness of my latter days; who had known all the murmurings of my heart!—How should I have lived in *your* remembrance!"

APRIL 28

Anne smiled and said, "My idea of good company, Mr. Elliot, is the company of clever, well-informed people, who have a great deal of conversation; that is what I call good company."

"You are mistaken," said he gently, "that is not good company, that is the best. Good company requires only birth, education and manners, and with regard to education is not very nice. Birth and good manners are essential; but a little learning is by no means a dangerous thing in good company, on the contrary, it will do very well."

APRIL 29

PRIDE AND PREJUDICE (1813),
JANE BENNET AND ELIZABETH BENNET

"It has been a very agreeable day," said Miss Bennet to Elizabeth. "The party seemed so well selected, so suitable one with the other. I hope we may often meet again."

Elizabeth smiled.

"Lizzy, you must not do so. You must not suspect me. It mortifies me. I assure you that I have now learnt to enjoy [Mr. Bingley's] conversation as an agreeable and sensible young man, without having a wish beyond it. I am perfectly satisfied from what his manners now are, that he never had any design of engaging my affection. It is only that he is blessed with greater sweetness of address, and a stronger desire of generally pleasing than any other man."

"You are very cruel," said her sister, "you will not let me smile, and are provoking me to it every moment."

"How hard it is in some cases to be believed!"

"And how impossible in others!"

"But why should you wish to persuade me that I feel more than I acknowledge?"

"That is a question which I hardly know how to answer. We all love to instruct, though we can teach only what is not worth knowing. Forgive me; and if you persist in indifference, do not make *me* your confidante."

APRIL 30

PERSUASION (1818), LADY RUSSELL TO ANNE ELLIOT

"We must be serious and decided—for, after all, the person who has contracted debts must pay them; and though a great deal is due to the feelings of the gentleman, and the head of a house, like your father, there is still more due to the character of an honest man."

MAY

"If there is no other objection to my marrying your nephew, I shall certainly not be kept from it, by knowing that his mother and aunt wished him to marry Miss De Bourgh. You both did as much as you could, in planning the marriage. Its completion depended on others. If Mr. Darcy is neither by honour nor inclination confined to his cousin, why is not he to make another choice? And if I am that choice, why may not I accept him?"

"Because honour, decorum, prudence, nay, interest, forbid it. Yes, Miss Bennet, interest; for do not expect to be noticed by his family or friends, if you wilfully act against the inclinations of all. You will be censured, slighted, and despised, by every one connected with him. Your alliance will be a disgrace; your name will never even be mentioned by any of us."

"These are heavy misfortunes," replied Elizabeth. "But the wife of Mr. Darcy must have such extraordinary sources of happiness necessarily attached to her situation, that she could, upon the whole, have no cause to repine."

"Obstinate, headstrong girl! I am ashamed of

you! Is this your gratitude for my attentions to you last spring? Is nothing due to me on that score?

"Let us sit down. You are to understand, Miss Bennet, that I came here with the determined resolution of carrying my purpose; nor will I be dissuaded from it. I have not been used to submit to any person's whims. I have not been in the habit of brooking disappointment."

"*That* will make your ladyship's situation at present more pitiable; but it will have no effect on *me*."

Pride and Prejudice (1813),
Elizabeth Bennet and Lady Catherine de Bourgh

MAY 1

"A married woman has many things to call her attention. I believe I was half an hour this morning shut up with my housekeeper."

MAY 2

Elizabeth continued her walk alone, crossing field after field at a quick pace, jumping over stiles and springing over puddles with impatient activity, and finding herself at last within view of the house, with weary ancles, dirty stockings, and a face glowing with the warmth of exercise.

MAY 3

They did not always think alike. His value for rank and connexion she perceived to be greater than hers.

She thanked him again and again; and with a sweetness of address which always attended her, invited him to be seated. But this he declined, as he was dirty and wet. Mrs. Dashwood then begged to know to whom she was obliged. His name, he replied, was Willoughby, and his present home was at Allenham, from whence he hoped she would allow him the honour of calling to-morrow to enquire after Miss Dashwood. The honour was readily granted, and he then departed, to make himself still more interesting, in the midst of an heavy rain.

MAY 5

PRIDE AND PREJUDICE (1813),
MRS. BENNET AND MR. BENNET

"You take delight in vexing me. You have no compassion on my poor nerves."

"You mistake me, my dear. I have a high respect for your nerves. They are my old friends. I have heard you mention them with consideration these twenty years at least."

MAY 6

"My sore-throats, you know, are always worse than anybody's."

MAY 7

"You think me foolish to call instruction a torment, but if you had been as much used as myself to hear poor little children first learning their letters and then learning to spell, if you had ever seen how stupid they can be for a whole morning together, and how tired my poor mother is at the end of it, as I am in the habit of seeing almost every day of my life at home, you would allow that to *torment* and to *instruct* might sometimes be used as synonimous words."

MAY 8

"Poverty is a great evil, but to a woman of education and feeling it ought not, it cannot be the greatest.— I would rather be a teacher at a school (and I can think of nothing worse) than marry a man I did not like.—"

MAY 9

A young woman, pretty, lively, with a harp as elegant as herself; and both placed near a window, cut down to the ground, and opening on a little lawn, surrounded by shrubs in the rich foliage of summer, was enough to catch any man's heart.

MAY 10

"Oh! go to-day, go to-day. Do not defer it. What is right to be done cannot be done too soon."

MAY 11

There certainly are not so many men of large fortune in the world, as there are pretty women to deserve them.

MAY 12

Fortunately for those who pay their court through such foibles, a fond mother, though, in pursuit of praise for her children, the most rapacious of human beings, is likewise the most credulous; her demands are exorbitant; but she will swallow any thing.

MAY 13

"I do not understand you."

"Then we are on very unequal terms, for I understand you perfectly well."

"Me?—yes; I cannot speak well enough to be unintelligible."

"Bravo!—an excellent satire on modern language."

"But pray tell me what you mean."

"Shall I indeed?—Do you really desire it?—But you are not aware of the consequences; it will involve you in a very cruel embarrassment, and certainly bring on a disagreement between us."

"No, no; it shall not do either; I am not afraid."

"Well then, I only meant that your attributing my brother's wish of dancing with Miss Thorpe to good-nature alone, convinced me of your being superior in good-nature yourself to all the rest of the world."

MAY 14

PRIDE AND PREJUDICE (1813),
ELIZABETH BENNET'S THOUGHTS ON MR. DARCY

Her heart did whisper, that he had done it for her. But it was a hope shortly checked by other considerations, and she soon felt that even her vanity was insufficient, when required to depend on his affection for her, for a woman who had already refused him.

MAY 15

PERSUASION (1818),
ADMIRAL CROFT TO ANNE ELLIOT

"One man's ways may be as good as another's, but we all like our own best."

MAY 16

SANDITON (1817)

Lady Denham, like a true great lady, talked and talked only of her own concerns.

"I cannot make speeches, Emma:"—he soon resumed; and in a tone of such sincere, decided, intelligible tenderness as was tolerably convincing.—"If I loved you less, I might be able to talk about it more. But you know what I am.—You hear nothing but truth from me.—I have blamed you, and lectured you, and you have borne it as no other woman in England would have borne it.—Bear with the truths I would tell you now, dearest Emma, as well as you have borne with them. The manner, perhaps, may have as little to recommend them. God knows, I have been a very indifferent lover.—But you understand me.—Yes, you see, you understand my feelings— and will return them if you can. At present, I ask only to hear, once to hear your voice."

"Selfishness must always be forgiven you know, because there is no hope of a cure."

"From the very beginning, from the first moment I may almost say, of my acquaintance with you, your manners impressing me with the fullest belief of your arrogance, your conceit, and your selfish disdain of the feelings of others, were such as to form that ground-work of disapprobation, on which succeeding events have built so immoveable a dislike; and I had not known you a month before I felt that you were the last man in the world whom I could ever be prevailed on to marry."

"You have said quite enough, madam. I perfectly comprehend your feelings, and have now only to be ashamed of what my own have been. Forgive me for having taken up so much of your time, and accept my best wishes for your health and happiness."

MAY 20

NORTHANGER ABBEY (1818)

A family of ten children will be always called a fine family, where there are heads and arms and legs enough for the number; but the Morlands had little other right to the word, for they were in general very plain, and Catherine, for many years of her life, as plain as any. She had a thin awkward figure, a sallow skin without colour, dark lank hair, and strong features;—so much for her person;—and not less unpropitious for heroism seemed her mind. She was fond of all boys' plays, and greatly preferred cricket not merely to dolls, but to the more heroic enjoyments of infancy, nursing a dormouse, feeding a canary-bird, or watering a rose-bush. Indeed she had no taste for a garden; and if she gathered flowers at all, it was chiefly for the pleasure of mischief— at least so it was conjectured from her always preferring those which she was forbidden to take.

MAY 21

PRIDE AND PREJUDICE (1813)

Bingley was ready, Georgiana was eager, and Darcy determined, to be pleased.

MAY 22

PRIDE AND PREJUDICE (1813),
MR. BENNET TO ELIZABETH BENNET

"Lizzy," said her father, "I have given him my consent. He is the kind of man, indeed, to whom I should never dare refuse any thing, which he condescended to ask. I now give it to *you*, if you are resolved on having him. But let me advise you to think better of it. I know your disposition, Lizzy. I know that you could be neither happy nor respectable, unless you truly esteemed your husband; unless you looked up to him as a superior. Your lively talents would place you in the greatest danger in an unequal marriage."

MAY 23

SENSE AND SENSIBILITY (1811), EDWARD FERRARS
TO ELINOR AND MARIANNE DASHWOOD

"I never wish to offend, but I am so foolishly shy, that I often seem negligent, when I am only kept back by my natural aukwardness. I have frequently thought that I must have been intended by nature to be fond of low company, I am so little at my ease among strangers of gentility!"

MAY 24

MANSFIELD PARK (1814)

From the time of their sitting down to table, it was a quick succession of busy nothings till the carriage came to the door.

PERSUASION (1818),

ADMIRAL CROFT TO ANNE ELLIOT

"I have done very little besides sending away some of the large looking-glasses from my dressing-room, which was your father's. A very good man, and very much the gentleman I am sure—but I should think, Miss Elliot" (looking with serious reflection) "I should think he must be rather a dressy man for his time of life.—Such a number of looking-glasses! oh Lord! there was no getting away from oneself. So I got Sophy to lend me a hand, and we soon shifted their quarters; and now I am quite snug, with my little shaving glass in one corner, and another great thing that I never go near."

MAY 26

EMMA (1816), MR. KNIGHTLEY

AND EMMA WOODHOUSE

"I do not understand what you mean by 'success;'" said Mr. Knightley. "Success supposes endeavour. Your time has been properly and delicately spent, if you have been endeavouring for the last four years to bring about this marriage. A worthy employment for a young lady's mind! But if, which I rather imagine, your making the match, as you call it, means only your planning it, your saying to yourself one idle day,

'I think it would be a very good thing for Miss Taylor if Mr. Weston were to marry her,' and saying it again to yourself every now and then afterwards,—why do you talk of success? where is your merit?—what are you proud of?—you made a lucky guess; and *that* is all that can be said."

"And have you never known the pleasure and triumph of a lucky guess?—I pity you.—I thought you cleverer—for depend upon it, a lucky guess is never merely luck. There is always some talent in it."

MAY 27

PERSUASION (1818)

Anne, at seven and twenty, thought very differently from what she had been made to think at nineteen.

MAY 28

PRIDE AND PREJUDICE (1813),
MR. DARCY TO ELIZABETH BENNET

"I have been a selfish being all my life, in practice, though not in principle."

MAY 29

"Know your own happiness. You want nothing but patience—or give it a more fascinating name, call it hope."

MAY 30

"The power of doing any thing with quickness is always much prized by the possessor, and often without any attention to the imperfection of the performance."

MAY 31

I will not say that your Mulberry trees are dead, but I am afraid they are not alive.

JUNE

"Lizzy declares she will not have Mr. Collins, and Mr. Collins begins to say that he will not have Lizzy."

"And what am I to do on the occasion?—It seems an hopeless business."

"Speak to Lizzy about it yourself. Tell her that you insist upon her marrying him."

"Let her be called down. She shall hear my opinion."

Mrs. Bennet rang the bell, and Miss Elizabeth was summoned to the library.

"Come here, child," cried her father as she appeared. "I have sent for you on an affair of importance. I understand that Mr. Collins has made you an offer of marriage. Is it true?" Elizabeth replied that it was. "Very well—and this offer of marriage you have refused?"

"I have, Sir."

"Very well. We now come to the point. Your mother insists upon your accepting it. Is not it so, Mrs. Bennet?"

"Yes, or I will never see her again."

"An unhappy alternative is before you, Elizabeth. From this day you must be a stranger to one of your parents.—Your mother will never see you again if

you do *not* marry Mr. Collins, and I will never see
you again if you *do*."

Pride and Prejudice (1813),
Mrs. Bennet and Mr. Bennet

৩৩৩

JUNE 1

SENSE AND SENSIBILITY (1811), ELINOR
DASHWOOD'S THOUGHTS ON MR. PALMER

His temper might perhaps be a little soured by finding, like many others of his sex, that through some unaccountable bias in favour of beauty, he was the husband of a very silly woman.

JUNE 2

THE WATSONS (C. 1803–5),
EMMA WATSON TO LORD OSBORNE

"Your Lordship thinks we always have our own way.—*That* is a point on which ladies and gentlemen have long disagreed.—But without pretending to decide it, I may say that there are some circumstances which even *women* cannot controul.—Female economy will do a great deal my Lord, but it cannot turn a small income into a large one."

JUNE 3

LETTER FROM JANE AUSTEN TO
CASSANDRA AUSTEN, 24–26 DECEMBER 1798,
ON MR. JOHN CALLAND

Mr Calland . . . appeared as usual with his hat in his

hand, & stood every now & then behind Catherine & me to be talked to & abused for not dancing.—We teized him however into it at last;—I was very glad to see him again after so long a separation, & he was altogether rather the Genius & Flirt of the Evening.

JUNE 4

PERSUASION (1818), ANNE ELLIOT'S THOUGHTS

While she considered Louisa to be rather the favourite, she could not but think, as far as she might dare to judge from memory and experience, that Captain Wentworth was not in love with either. They were more in love with him; yet there it was not love. It was a little fever of admiration; but it might, probably must, end in love with some.

JUNE 5

EMMA (1816), EMMA WOODHOUSE'S
THOUGHTS ON MRS. ELTON

She did not really like her. She would not be in a hurry to find fault, but she suspected that there was no elegance;—ease, but not elegance.—She was almost sure that for a young woman, a stranger, a bride, there was too much ease.

JUNE 6

A house was never taken good care of, Mr. Shepherd observed, without a lady: he did not know, whether furniture might not be in danger of suffering as much where there was no lady, as where there were many children. A lady, without a family, was the very best preserver of furniture in the world.

JUNE 7

She was moreover noisy and wild, hated confinement and cleanliness, and loved nothing so well in the world as rolling down the green slope at the back of the house.

Such was Catherine Morland at ten.

JUNE 8

A mind lively and at ease, can do with seeing nothing, and can see nothing that does not answer.

"Women may be as comfortable on board [a ship], as in the best house in England. I believe I have lived as much on board as most women, and I know nothing superior to the accommodations of a man of war."

"Oh! yes, I am quite aware of that. It is the garden of England, you know. Surry is the garden of England."

"Yes; but we must not rest our claims on that distinction. Many counties, I believe, are called the garden of England, as well as Surry."

"No, I fancy not," replied Mrs. Elton, with a most satisfied smile. "I never heard any county but Surry called so."

Her brother was not handsome; no, when they first saw him, he was absolutely plain, black and plain; but still he was the gentleman, with a pleasing address. The second meeting proved him not so very plain; he was plain, to be sure, but then he had so much countenance, and his teeth were so good, and he was so well made, that one soon forgot he was plain; and after a third interview, after dining in company with him at the parsonage, he was no longer allowed to be called so by any body. He was, in fact, the most agreeable young man the sisters had ever known, and they were equally delighted with him. Miss Bertram's engagement made him in equity the property of Julia, of which Julia was fully aware, and before he had been at Mansfield a week, she was quite ready to be fallen in love with.

JUNE 12

SENSE AND SENSIBILITY (1811),
ELINOR DASHWOOD AND MARIANNE DASHWOOD

"Do you compare your conduct with his?"

"No. I compare it with what it ought to have been; I compare it with yours."

JUNE 13

PERSUASION (1818), ON CAPTAIN BENWICK

He had an affectionate heart. He must love somebody.

JUNE 14

SENSE AND SENSIBILITY (1811), MARIANNE
DASHWOOD TO ELINOR DASHWOOD

"A man who has nothing to do with his own time has no conscience in his intrusion on that of others."

JUNE 15

LETTER FROM JANE AUSTEN TO
CASSANDRA AUSTEN, 15–17 JUNE 1808

Where shall I begin? Which of all my important nothings shall I tell you first?

JUNE 16

LETTER FROM JANE AUSTEN TO
CASSANDRA AUSTEN, 15–17 JUNE 1808

You know how interesting the purchase of a sponge-cake is to me.

JUNE 17

"There is hardly any personal defect," replied Anne, "which an agreeable manner might not gradually reconcile one to."

JUNE 18

Not all that Mrs. Bennet, however, with the assistance of her five daughters, could ask on the subject was sufficient to draw from her husband any satisfactory description of Mr. Bingley. They attacked him in various ways; with barefaced questions, ingenious suppositions, and distant surmises; but he eluded the skill of them all; and they were at last obliged to accept the second-hand intelligence of their neighbour.

JUNE 19

"Yes," said Anne, "you tell me nothing which does not accord with what I have known, or could imagine. There is always something offensive in the details of cunning. The manoeuvres of selfishness and duplicity must ever be revolting, but I have heard nothing which really surprises me. I know those who would be shocked by such a representation of Mr. Elliot, who would have difficulty in believing it; but I have never been satisfied. I have always wanted some other motive for his conduct than appeared."

JUNE 20

JACK AND ALICE (C. 1790)

The perfect form, the beautifull face, and elegant manners of Lucy so won on the affections of Alice that when they parted, which was not till after Supper, she assured her that except her Father, Brother, Uncles, Aunts, Cousins and other relations, Lady Williams, Charles Adams and a few dozen more of particular freinds, she loved her better than almost any other person in the world.

Such a flattering assurance of her regard would justly have given much pleasure to the object of it, had she not plainly perceived that the amiable Alice had partaken too freely of Lady Williams's claret.

JUNE 21

To look *almost* pretty, is an acquisition of higher delight to a girl who has been looking plain the first fifteen years of her life, than a beauty from her cradle can ever receive.

JUNE 22

It darted through her, with the speed of an arrow, that Mr. Knightley must marry no one but herself!

JUNE 23

Here was that elasticity of mind, that disposition to be comforted, that power of turning readily from evil to good, and of finding employment which carried her out of herself, which was from Nature alone. It was the choicest gift of Heaven; and Anne viewed her friend as one of those instances in which, by a merciful appointment, it seems designed to counterbalance almost every other want.

JUNE 24

"Insufferable woman!" was her immediate exclamation. "Worse than I had supposed. Absolutely insufferable! Knightley!—I could not have believed it. Knightley!—never seen him in her life before, and call him Knightley!—and discover that he is a gentleman! A little upstart, vulgar being, with her Mr. E., and her *cara sposo*, and her resources, and all her airs of pert pretension and under-bred finery. Actually to discover that Mr. Knightley is a gentleman! I doubt whether he will return the compliment, and discover her to be a lady."

JUNE 25

"I consider a country-dance as an emblem of marriage. Fidelity and complaisance are the principal duties of both; and those men who do not chuse to dance or marry themselves, have no business with the partners or wives of their neighbours."

"But they are such very different things!—"

"—That you think they cannot be compared together."

"To be sure not. People that marry can never

part, but must go and keep house together. People that dance, only stand opposite each other in a long room for half an hour."

"And such is your definition of matrimony and dancing. Taken in that light certainly, their resemblance is not striking; but I think I could place them in such a view.—You will allow, that in both, man has the advantage of choice, woman only the power of refusal."

JUNE 26
MANSFIELD PARK (1814)

It would not be fair to enquire into a young lady's exact estimate of her own perfections.

JUNE 27
SENSE AND SENSIBILITY (1811),
ELINOR DASHWOOD'S THOUGHTS

"I *will* be calm; I *will* be mistress of myself."

JUNE 28
EMMA (1816)

The wedding was very much like other weddings,

where the parties have no taste for finery or parade; and Mrs. Elton, from the particulars detailed by her husband, thought it all extremely shabby, and very inferior to her own.—"Very little white satin, very few lace veils; a most pitiful business!—Selina would stare when she heard of it."—But, in spite of these deficiencies, the wishes, the hopes, the confidence, the predictions of the small band of true friends who witnessed the ceremony, were fully answered in the perfect happiness of the union.

JUNE 29

PERSUASION (1818)

Husbands and wives generally understand when opposition will be vain.

JUNE 30

PRIDE AND PREJUDICE (1813),
MR. BENNET TO ELIZABETH BENNET

"So, Lizzy," said he one day, "your sister is crossed in love I find. I congratulate her. Next to being married, a girl likes to be crossed in love a little now and then. It is something to think of, and gives her a sort of distinction among her companions. When is your turn to come? You will hardly bear to be long outdone by Jane. Now is your time. Here are officers enough at Meryton to disappoint all the young ladies in the country. Let Wickham be *your* man. He is a pleasant fellow, and would jilt you creditably."

JULY

"Yes, I am fond of history."

"I wish I were too. I read it a little as a duty, but it tells me nothing that does not either vex or weary me. The quarrels of popes and kings, with wars or pestilences, in every page; the men all so good for nothing, and hardly any women at all—it is very tiresome: and yet I often think it odd that it should be so dull, for a great deal of it must be invention. The speeches that are put into the heroes' mouths, their thoughts and designs—the chief of all this must be invention, and invention is what delights me in other books."

"Historians, you think," said Miss Tilney, "are not happy in their flights of fancy. They display imagination without raising interest. I am fond of history—and am very well contented to take the false with the true. In the principal facts they have sources of intelligence in former histories and records, which may be as much depended on, I conclude, as any thing that does not actually pass under one's own observation; and as for the little embellishments you speak of, they are embellishments, and I like them as such. If a speech be well drawn up, I read it with pleasure, by whomsoever it may be made—and probably with much greater, if the production of Mr. Hume or Mr. Robertson, than if the genuine words of Caractacus, Agricola, or Alfred the Great."

"You are fond of history!—and so are Mr. Allen and my father; and I have two brothers who do not dislike it. So many instances within my small circle of friends is remarkable! At this rate, I shall not pity the writers of history any longer. If people like to read their books, it is all very well, but to be at so much trouble in filling great volumes, which, as I used to think, nobody would willingly ever look into, to be labouring only for the torment of little boys and girls, always struck me as a hard fate; and though I know it is all very right and necessary, I have often wondered at the person's courage that could sit down on purpose to do it."

Northanger Abbey (1818),
Eleanor Tilney and Catherine Morland

"Letters are no matter of indifference; they are generally a very positive curse."

"You are speaking of letters of business; mine are letters of friendship."

"I have often thought them the worst of the two," replied he coolly. "Business, you know, may bring money, but friendship hardly ever does."

"Ah! you are not serious now. I know Mr. John Knightley too well—I am very sure he understands the value of friendship as well as any body. I can easily believe that letters are very little to you, much less than to me, but it is not your being ten years older than myself which makes the difference, it is not age, but situation. You have every body dearest to you always at hand, I, probably, never shall again; and therefore till I have outlived all my affections, a post-office, I think, must always have power to draw me out, in worse weather than to-day."

"Surprizes are foolish things. The pleasure is not enhanced, and the inconvenience is often considerable."

JULY 3

"Now I must give one smirk, and then we may be rational again."

JULY 4

She gloried in being a sailor's wife, but she must pay the tax of quick alarm for belonging to that profession which is, if possible, more distinguished in its domestic virtues than in its national importance.

JULY 5

Miss Hawkins was the youngest of the two daughters of a Bristol—merchant, of course, he must be called; but, as the whole of the profits of his mercantile life appeared so very moderate, it was not unfair to guess the dignity of his line of trade had been very moderate also. Part of every winter she had been used to spend in Bath; but Bristol was her home, the very heart of Bristol; for though the father and mother had died some years ago, an uncle remained—in the law line—nothing more distinctly honourable was hazarded of him, than that he was in the law line; and with him the daughter had lived. Emma guessed him to be the drudge of some attorney, and too stupid to rise. And all the grandeur of the connection seemed dependent on the elder sister, who was *very well married*, to a gentleman in a *great way*, near Bristol, who kept two carriages! That was the wind-up of the history; that was the glory of Miss Hawkins.

JULY 6

PRIDE AND PREJUDICE (1813),
MR. DARCY TO ELIZABETH BENNET

"In vain have I struggled. It will not do. My feelings will not be repressed. You must allow me to tell you how ardently I admire and love you."

JULY 7

MANSFIELD PARK (1814),
FANNY PRICE TO MARY CRAWFORD

"I was quiet, but I was not blind. I could not but see that Mr. Crawford allowed himself in gallantries which did mean nothing."

"It was, perhaps, one of those cases in which advice is good or bad only as the event decides."

"We have all a better guide in ourselves, if we would attend to it, than any other person can be."

Lady Middleton resigned herself to the idea of it, with all the philosophy of a well bred woman, contenting herself with merely giving her husband a gentle reprimand on the subject five or six times every day.

JULY 11

JACK AND ALICE (C. 1790),
LADY WILLIAMS TO ALICE JOHNSON

"Preserve yourself from a first Love and you need not fear a second."

JULY 12

PERSUASION (1818), ON CAPTAIN WENTWORTH

He was only wrong in accepting the attentions—(for accepting must be the word) of two young women at once.

JULY 13

PRIDE AND PREJUDICE (1813),
CHARLOTTE LUCAS TO ELIZABETH BENNET

"There are very few of us who have heart enough to be really in love without encouragement."

JULY 14

EMMA (1816)

Emma Woodhouse, handsome, clever, and rich, with a comfortable home and happy disposition, seemed to unite some of the best blessings of existence; and had lived nearly twenty-one years in the world with very little to distress or vex her.

JULY 15

EMMA (1816), MR. KNIGHTLEY
TO EMMA WOODHOUSE, ON MISS BATES

"Were she your equal in situation—but, Emma, consider how far this is from being the case. She is poor; she has sunk from the comforts she was born to; and, if she live to old age, must probably sink more. Her situation should secure your compassion. It was badly done, indeed!"

JULY 16

PRIDE AND PREJUDICE (1813),
MR. DARCY TO CAROLINE BINGLEY

"I cannot comprehend the neglect of a family library in such days as these."

JULY 17

PERSUASION (1818), ON ANNE ELLIOT

Anne hoped she had outlived the age of blushing; but the age of emotion she certainly had not.

She felt herself to be dying about half an hour before she became tranquil & aparently unconscious. During that half hour was her struggle, poor Soul! she said she could not tell us what she sufferd, tho she complaind of little fixed pain. When I asked her if there was any thing she wanted, her answer was she wanted nothing but death & some of her words were "God grant me patience, Pray for me Oh Pray for me". Her voice was affected but as long as she spoke she was intelligible. I hope I do not break your heart my dearest Fanny by these particulars.

"If any one faculty of our nature may be called *more* wonderful than the rest, I do think it is memory. There seems something more speakingly incomprehensible in the powers, the failures, the inequalities of memory, than in any other of our intelligences. The memory is sometimes so retentive, so serviceable, so obedient—at others, so bewildered and so weak—and at others again, so tyrannic, so beyond controul!—We are to be sure a miracle every way—but our powers of recollecting and of forgetting, do seem peculiarly past finding out."

Mrs. Morland was a very good woman, and wished to see her children every thing they ought to be; but her time was so much occupied in lying-in and teaching the little ones, that her elder daughters were inevitably left to shift for themselves; and it was not very wonderful that Catherine, who had by nature nothing heroic about her, should prefer cricket, base ball, riding on horseback, and running about the country at the age of fourteen, to books—or at least books of information—for, provided that nothing like useful knowledge could be gained from them, provided they were all story and no reflection, she had never any objection to books at all. But from fifteen to seventeen she was in training for a heroine; she read all such works as heroines must read to supply their memories with those quotations which are so serviceable and so soothing in the vicissitudes of their eventful lives.

JULY 21

She was not a woman of many words: for, unlike people in general, she proportioned them to the number of her ideas.

JULY 22

I leave it to be settled by whomsoever it may concern, whether the tendency of this work be altogether to recommend parental tyranny, or reward filial disobedience.

JULY 23

She had prejudices on the side of ancestry; she had a value for rank and consequence, which blinded her a little to the faults of those who possessed them.

JULY 24

"Ah! there is nothing like staying at home, for real comfort. Nobody can be more devoted to home than

I am. I was quite a proverb for it at Maple Grove. Many a time has Selina said, when she has been going to Bristol, 'I really cannot get this girl to move from the house. I absolutely must go in by myself, though I hate being stuck up in the barouche-landau without a companion; but Augusta, I believe, with her own good will, would never stir beyond the park paling.' Many a time has she said so; and yet I am no advocate for entire seclusion. I think, on the contrary, when people shut themselves up entirely from society, it is a very bad thing; and that it is much more advisable to mix in the world in a proper degree, without living in it either too much or too little."

JULY 25

MANSFIELD PARK (1814), ON SIR THOMAS BERTRAM

Sir Thomas saw repeated, and for ever repeated reason to rejoice in what he had done for them all, and acknowledge the advantages of early hardship and discipline, and the consciousness of being born to struggle and endure.

JULY 26

PERSUASION (1818), ON ANNE ELLIOT

Anne, with an elegance of mind and sweetness of character, which must have placed her high with any people of real understanding, was nobody with either father or sister: her word had no weight; her convenience was always to give way;—she was only Anne.

"You may imagine that I am happy on every occasion to offer those little delicate compliments which are always acceptable to ladies. I have more than once observed to Lady Catherine, that her charming daughter seemed born to be a duchess, and that the most elevated rank, instead of giving her consequence, would be adorned by her.—These are the kind of little things which please her ladyship, and it is a sort of attention which I conceive myself peculiarly bound to pay."

"You judge very properly," said Mr. Bennet, "and it is happy for you that you possess the talent of flattering with delicacy. May I ask whether these pleasing attentions proceed from the impulse of the moment, or are the result of previous study?"

"They arise chiefly from what is passing at the time, and though I sometimes amuse myself with suggesting and arranging such little elegant compliments as may be adapted to ordinary occasions, I always wish to give them as unstudied an air as possible."

Mr. Bennet's expectations were fully answered. His cousin was as absurd as he had hoped, and he listened to him with the keenest enjoyment.

JULY 28

She had given him up to oblige others. It had been the effect of over-persuasion. It had been weakness and timidity.

JULY 29

"Your conjecture is totally wrong, I assure you. My mind was more agreeably engaged. I have been meditating on the very great pleasure which a pair of fine eyes in the face of a pretty woman can bestow."

"I think you must like Udolpho, if you were to read it; it is so very interesting."

"Not I, faith! No, if I read any, it shall be Mrs. Radcliff's; her novels are amusing enough; they are worth reading; some fun and nature in *them*."

"Udolpho was written by Mrs. Radcliff," said Catherine, with some hesitation, from the fear of mortifying him.

"No sure; was it? Aye, I remember, so it was; I was thinking of that other stupid book, written by that woman they make such a fuss about, she who married the French emigrant."

"I suppose you mean Camilla?"

"Yes, that's the book; such unnatural stuff!—An old man playing at see-saw! I took up the first volume once and looked it over, but I soon found it would not do; indeed I guessed what sort of stuff it must be before I saw it: as soon as I heard she had married an emigrant, I was sure I should never be able to get through it."

"I must have my share in the conversation, if you are speaking of music. There are few people in England, I suppose, who have more true enjoyment of music than myself, or a better natural taste. If I had ever learnt, I should have been a great proficient."

AUGUST

"For my own part," she rejoined, "I must confess that I never could see any beauty in her. Her face is too thin; her complexion has no brilliancy; and her features are not at all handsome. Her nose wants character; there is nothing marked in its lines. Her teeth are tolerable, but not out of the common way; and as for her eyes, which have sometimes been called so fine, I never could perceive any thing extraordinary in them. They have a sharp, shrewish look, which I do not like at all; and in her air altogether, there is a self-sufficiency without fashion, which is intolerable."

Persuaded as Miss Bingley was that Darcy admired Elizabeth, this was not the best method of recommending herself; but angry people are not always wise; and in seeing him at last look somewhat nettled, she had all the success she expected. He was resolutely silent however; and, from a determination of making him speak, she continued,

"I remember, when we first knew her in Hertfordshire, how amazed we all were to find that she was a reputed beauty; and I particularly recollect your saying one night, after they had been dining at Netherfield, '*She* a beauty!—I should as soon call her mother a wit.' But afterwards she seemed to improve on you, and I believe you thought her rather pretty at one time."

"Yes," replied Darcy, who could contain himself no longer, "but *that* was only when I first knew her, for it is many months since I have considered her as one of the handsomest women of my acquaintance."

He then went away, and Miss Bingley was left to all the satisfaction of having forced him to say what gave no one any pain but herself.

Pride and Prejudice (1813),
Caroline Bingley and Mr. Darcy

AUGUST 1

LETTER FROM JANE AUSTEN TO
CASSANDRA AUSTEN, 18 SEPTEMBER 1796

What dreadful Hot weather we have!—It keeps one
in a continual state of Inelegance.

AUGUST 2

THE WATSONS (C. 1803–5),
EMMA WATSON'S THOUGHTS

She was beginning to feel that a family party might
be the worst of all parties.

AUGUST 3

THE HISTORY OF ENGLAND (C. 1791)

Edward the 4th. . . . One of Edward's Mistresses was
Jane Shore, who has had a play written about her,
but it is a tragedy and therefore not worth reading.

AUGUST 4

LETTER FROM JANE AUSTEN TO
CASSANDRA AUSTEN, 24 JANUARY 1809

Your silence on the subject of our Ball, makes me suppose your Curiosity too great for words.

AUGUST 5

NORTHANGER ABBEY (1818),
CATHERINE MORLAND AND ISABELLA THORPE

"Scold them! Do you scold them for not admiring her?"

"Yes, that I do. There is nothing I would not do for those who are really my friends. I have no notion of loving people by halves, it is not my nature. My attachments are always excessively strong. I told Capt. Hunt at one of our assemblies this winter, that if he was to tease me all night, I would not dance with him, unless he would allow Miss Andrews to be as beautiful as an angel. The men think us incapable of real friendship you know, and I am determined to shew them the difference. Now, if I were to hear any body speak slightingly of you, I should fire up in a moment:—but that is not at all likely, for *you* are just the kind of girl to be a great favourite with the men."

"Oh! dear," cried Catherine, colouring, "how can you say so?"

"I know you very well; you have so much animation, which is exactly what Miss Andrews wants, for I must confess there is something amazingly insipid about her."

AUGUST 6

EMMA (1816), MISS BATES TO ALL

"I will not positively answer for my having never dropt a hint, because I know I do sometimes pop out a thing before I am aware. I am a talker, you know; I am rather a talker; and now and then I have let a thing escape me which I should not. I am not like Jane; I wish I were. I will answer for it *she* never betrayed the least thing in the world. Where is she?—Oh! just behind."

AUGUST 7

PRIDE AND PREJUDICE (1813), MARY BENNET
TO ELIZABETH BENNET AND OTHERS

"Vanity and pride are different things, though the words are often used synonimously. A person may be proud without being vain. Pride relates more to our opinion of ourselves, vanity to what we would have others think of us."

AUGUST 8

"They are much to be pitied who have not been taught to feel in some degree as you do—who have not at least been given a taste for nature in early life. They lose a great deal."

"*You* taught me to think and feel on the subject, cousin."

"I had a very apt scholar."

AUGUST 9

To flatter and follow others, without being flattered and followed in turn, is but a state of half enjoyment.

AUGUST 10

It was soon pain upon pain, confusion upon confusion; for they were hardly in the High Street, before they met [Fanny Price's] father, whose appearance was not the better from its being Saturday. He stopt; and, ungentlemanlike as he looked, Fanny was obliged to introduce him to Mr. Crawford. She could not have a doubt of the manner in which Mr. Crawford must be struck. He must be ashamed and disgusted altogether. He must soon give her up, and cease to have the smallest inclination for the match; and yet, though she had been so much wanting his affection to be cured, this was a sort of cure that would be almost as bad as the complaint; and I believe, there is scarcely a young lady in the united kingdoms, who would not rather put up with the misfortune of being sought by a clever, agreeable man, than have him driven away by the vulgarity of her nearest relations.

AUGUST 11

PRIDE AND PREJUDICE (1813), MRS. BENNET AND MR. BENNET TO ELIZABETH BENNET

"My dearest child," she cried, "I can think of nothing else! Ten thousand a year, and very likely more! 'Tis as good as a Lord! And a special licence. You must and shall be married by a special licence. But my dearest love, tell me what dish Mr. Darcy is particularly fond of, that I may have it to-morrow."

This was a sad omen of what her mother's behaviour to the gentleman himself might be; and Elizabeth found, that though in the certain possession of his warmest affection, and secure of her relations' consent, there was still something to be wished for. But the morrow passed off much better than she expected; for Mrs. Bennet luckily stood in such awe of her intended son-in-law, that she ventured not to speak to him, unless it was in her power to offer him any attention, or mark her deference for his opinion.

Elizabeth had the satisfaction of seeing her father taking pains to get acquainted with him; and Mr. Bennet soon assured her that he was rising every hour in his esteem.

"I admire all my three sons-in-law highly," said he. "Wickham, perhaps, is my favourite; but I think I shall like *your* husband quite as well as Jane's."

AUGUST 12

PERSUASION (1818), ON ANNE ELLIOT

When the evening was over, Anne could not but be amused at the idea of her coming to Lyme, to preach patience and resignation to a young man whom she had never seen before; nor could she help fearing, on more serious reflection, that, like many other great moralists and preachers, she had been eloquent on a point in which her own conduct would ill bear examination.

AUGUST 13

Self-interest alone could induce a woman to keep
a man to an engagement, of which she seemed so
thoroughly aware that he was weary.

AUGUST 14

If I *am* a wild Beast, I cannot help it. It is not my
own fault.

AUGUST 15

"A woman can never be too fine while she is all in
white."

AUGUST 16

"And yet I meant to be uncommonly clever in taking

so decided a dislike to him, without any reason. It is such a spur to one's genius, such an opening for wit to have a dislike of that kind. One may be continually abusive without saying any thing just; but one cannot be always laughing at a man without now and then stumbling on something witty."

AUGUST 17

PRIDE AND PREJUDICE (1813),
ELIZABETH BENNET AND MRS. GARDINER

"Stupid men are the only ones worth knowing, after all."

"Take care, Lizzy; that speech savours strongly of disappointment."

AUGUST 18

PRIDE AND PREJUDICE (1813),
ELIZABETH BENNET TO MRS. GARDINER

"You give me fresh life and vigour. Adieu to disappointment and spleen. What are men to rocks and mountains? Oh! what hours of transport we shall spend! And when we *do* return, it shall not be like other travellers, without being able to give one accurate idea of any thing. We *will* know where we have gone—we *will* recollect what we have seen. Lakes, mountains, and rivers, shall not be jumbled together in our imaginations; nor, when we attempt to describe any particular scene, will we begin quarrelling about its relative situation. Let *our* first effusions be less insupportable than those of the generality of travellers."

"Eliza Bennet," said Miss Bingley, when the door was closed on her, "is one of those young ladies who seek to recommend themselves to the other sex, by undervaluing their own; and with many men, I dare say, it succeeds. But, in my opinion, it is a paltry device, a very mean art."

"Undoubtedly," replied Darcy, to whom this remark was chiefly addressed, "there is meanness in *all* the arts which ladies sometimes condescend to employ for captivation. Whatever bears affinity to cunning is despicable."

Miss Bingley was not so entirely satisfied with this reply as to continue the subject.

Elizabeth's spirits soon rising to playfulness again,

she wanted Mr. Darcy to account for his having ever fallen in love with her. "How could you begin?" said she. "I can comprehend your going on charmingly, when you had once made a beginning; but what could set you off in the first place?"

"I cannot fix on the hour, or the spot, or the look, or the words, which laid the foundation. It is too long ago. I was in the middle before I knew that I *had* begun."

"My beauty you had early withstood, and as for my manners—my behaviour to *you* was at least always bordering on the uncivil, and I never spoke to you without rather wishing to give you pain than not. Now be sincere; did you admire me for my impertinence?"

"For the liveliness of your mind, I did."

"You may as well call it impertinence at once. It was very little less. The fact is, that you were sick of civility, of deference, of officious attention. You were disgusted with the women who were always speaking and looking, and thinking for *your* approbation alone. I roused, and interested you, because I was so unlike *them*."

AUGUST 21

MANSFIELD PARK (1814)

There is nothing like employment, active, indispensable employment, for relieving sorrow.

AUGUST 22

PRIDE AND PREJUDICE (1813)

Happy for all her maternal feelings was the day on which Mrs. Bennet got rid of her two most deserving daughters.

AUGUST 23

LETTER FROM JANE AUSTEN TO
CASSANDRA AUSTEN, 23 AUGUST 1796

Here I am once more in this Scene of Dissipation & vice, and I begin already to find my Morals corrupted.

AUGUST 24

MANSFIELD PARK (1814),
EDMUND BERTRAM TO FANNY PRICE

"Good-humoured, unaffected girls, will not do for a man who has been used to sensible women. They are two distinct orders of being."

AUGUST 25

PRIDE AND PREJUDICE (1813),
JANE BENNET TO ELIZABETH BENNET

"Laugh as much as you chuse, but you will not laugh me out of my opinion."

AUGUST 26

PRIDE AND PREJUDICE (1813), ELIZABETH BENNET
TO LADY CATHERINE DE BOURGH, ON MR. DARCY

"He is a gentleman; I am a gentleman's daughter; so far we are equal."

AUGUST 27

MANSFIELD PARK (1814), FANNY PRICE'S THOUGHTS

Her own thoughts and reflections were habitually her best companions.

AUGUST 28

PRIDE AND PREJUDICE (1813),
MR. DARCY TO ELIZABETH BENNET

"We neither of us perform to strangers."

AUGUST 29

Elinor's security sunk; but her self-command did not sink with it.

AUGUST 30

"A large income is the best recipé for happiness I ever heard of."

AUGUST 31

To come with a well-informed mind, is to come with an inability of administering to the vanity of others, which a sensible person would always wish to avoid. A woman especially, if she have the misfortune of knowing any thing, should conceal it as well as she can.

SEPTEMBER

Emma was sorry;—to have to pay civilities to a person she did not like through three long months!—to be always doing more than she wished, and less than she ought! Why she did not like Jane Fairfax might be a difficult question to answer; Mr. Knightley had once told her it was because she saw in her the really accomplished young woman, which she wanted to be thought herself; and though the accusation had been eagerly refuted at the time, there were moments of self-examination in which her conscience could not quite acquit her. But "she could never get acquainted with her: she did not know how it was, but there was such coldness and reserve—such apparent indifference whether she pleased or not—and then, her aunt was such an eternal talker! —and she was made such a fuss with by every body!—and it had been always imagined that they were to be so intimate—because their ages were the same, every body had supposed they must be so fond of each other." These were her reasons—she had no better.

It was a dislike so little just—every imputed fault was so magnified by fancy, that she never saw Jane

Fairfax the first time after any considerable absence, without feeling that she had injured her.

Emma (1816)

SEPTEMBER 1

LETTER FROM JANE AUSTEN TO
CASSANDRA AUSTEN, 1 SEPTEMBER 1796

The letter which I have this moment received from you has diverted me beyond moderation. I could die of laughter at it, as they used to say at school. You are indeed the finest comic writer of the present age.

SEPTEMBER 2

EMMA (1816), EMMA WOODHOUSE
AND MR. KNIGHTLEY, ON HARRIET SMITH

"I am very much mistaken if your sex in general would not think such beauty, and such temper, the highest claims a woman could possess."

"Upon my word, Emma, to hear you abusing the reason you have, is almost enough to make me think so too. Better be without sense, than misapply it as you do."

SEPTEMBER 3

MANSFIELD PARK (1814), MRS. RUSHWORTH,
ON HENRY CRAWFORD

"Those who have not more, must be satisfied with what they have."

SEPTEMBER 4

PERSUASION (1818)

Personal size and mental sorrow have certainly no necessary proportions. A large bulky figure has as good a right to be in deep affliction, as the most graceful set of limbs in the world. But, fair or not fair, there are unbecoming conjunctions, which reason will patronize in vain,—which taste cannot tolerate,—which ridicule will seize.

SEPTEMBER 5

LETTER FROM JANE AUSTEN TO
CASSANDRA AUSTEN, 5 SEPTEMBER 1796

Mr Richard Harvey is going to be married; but as it is a great secret, & only known to half the Neighbourhood, you must not mention it. The Lady's name is Musgrove.

SEPTEMBER 6

PERSUASION (1818), SIR WALTER ELLIOT
AND ADMIRAL CROFT

Sir Walter, without hesitation, declared the Admiral to be the best-looking sailor he had ever met with, and went so far as to say, that, if his own man might have had the arranging of his hair, he should not be ashamed of being seen with him any where; and the Admiral, with sympathetic cordiality, observed to his wife as they drove back through the Park, "I thought we should soon come to a deal, my dear, in spite of what they told us at Taunton. The baronet will never set the Thames on fire, but there seems no harm in him:"—reciprocal compliments, which would have been esteemed about equal.

SEPTEMBER 7

SENSE AND SENSIBILITY (1811), MARIANNE
DASHWOOD AND EDWARD FERRARS

"How can you think of dirt, with such objects before you?"

"Because," replied he, smiling, "among the rest of the objects before me, I see a very dirty lane."

SEPTEMBER 8

PRIDE AND PREJUDICE (1813), JANE BENNET AND
ELIZABETH BENNET, ON MR. DARCY

"Will you tell me how long you have loved him?"

"It has been coming on so gradually, that I hardly know when it began. But I believe I must date it from my first seeing his beautiful grounds at Pemberley."

Another intreaty that she would be serious, however, produced the desired effect; and she soon satisfied Jane by her solemn assurances of attachment.

SEPTEMBER 9

LETTER FROM JANE AUSTEN TO
ANNA AUSTEN, 9–18 SEPTEMBER 1814

You are now collecting your People delightfully, getting them exactly into such a spot as is the delight of my life;—3 or 4 Families in a Country Village is the very thing to work on—& I hope you will write a great deal more, & make full use of them while they are so very favourably arranged. You are but *now* coming to the heart & beauty of your book; till the heroine grows up, the fun must be imperfect—but I expect a great deal of entertainment from the next 3 or 4 books, & I hope you will not resent these remarks by sending me no more.

SEPTEMBER 10

MANSFIELD PARK (1814), MARY CRAWFORD
WRITING TO FANNY PRICE

"Varnish and gilding hide many stains."

SEPTEMBER 11

NORTHANGER ABBEY (1818)

What young lady of common gentility will reach the age of sixteen without altering her name as far as she can?

SEPTEMBER 12

PRIDE AND PREJUDICE (1813),
MR. BENNET TO ELIZABETH BENNET

"For what do we live, but to make sport for our neighbours, and laugh at them in our turn?"

SEPTEMBER 13

PRIDE AND PREJUDICE (1813),
MR. DARCY TO ELIZABETH BENNET

"Nothing is more deceitful," said Darcy, "than the appearance of humility. It is often only carelessness of opinion, and sometimes an indirect boast."

SEPTEMBER 14

SANDITON (1817),
CHARLOTTE HEYWOOD'S THOUGHTS

"Thus it is, when rich people are sordid."

SEPTEMBER 15

EMMA (1816)

The ladies here probably exchanged looks which meant, "Men never know when things are dirty or not;" and the gentlemen perhaps thought each to himself, "Women will have their little nonsenses and needless cares."

SEPTEMBER 16

LETTER FROM JANE AUSTEN TO
CASSANDRA AUSTEN, 5 SEPTEMBER 1796

Pray remember me to Everybody who does not enquire after me. Those who do, remember me without bidding.

SEPTEMBER 17

"I hate the idea of one great fortune looking out for another. And to marry for money I think the wickedest thing in existence."

SEPTEMBER 18

How ill I have written. I begin to hate myself. Y^{rs} ever—J: Austen—

SEPTEMBER 19

As far as walking, talking, and contriving reached, she was thoroughly benevolent, and nobody knew better how to dictate liberality to others: but her love of money was equal to her love of directing, and she knew quite as well how to save her own as to spend that of her friends.

SEPTEMBER 20

LETTER FROM JANE AUSTEN TO
FANNY KNIGHT, 18–20 NOVEMBER 1814

Wisdom is better than Wit, & in the long run will certainly have the laugh on her side.

SEPTEMBER 21

PRIDE AND PREJUDICE (1813),
MR. DARCY TO ELIZABETH BENNET

"Mr. Wickham is blessed with such happy manners as may ensure his *making* friends—whether he may be equally capable of *retaining* them, is less certain."

SEPTEMBER 22

MANSFIELD PARK (1814), MARY CRAWFORD
TO WILLIAM PRICE AND OTHERS

"There, I will stake my last like a woman of spirit. No cold prudence for me. I am not born to sit still and do nothing. If I lose the game, it shall not be from not striving for it."

"Those who tell their own story you know must be listened to with caution."

Even in the midst of his late infatuation, he had acknowledged Fanny's mental superiority. What must be his sense of it now, therefore? She was of course only too good for him; but as nobody minds having what is too good for them, he was very steadily earnest in the pursuit of the blessing, and it was not possible that encouragement from her should be long wanting.

I do not want People to be very agreable, as it saves me the trouble of liking them a great deal.

SEPTEMBER 26

"I hope I never ridicule what is wise or good. Follies and nonsense, whims and inconsistencies *do* divert me, I own, and I laugh at them whenever I can."

SEPTEMBER 27

"Oh! I am not at all afraid of her dying. People do not die of little trifling colds."

SEPTEMBER 28

"Money can only give happiness where there is nothing else to give it."

"They who are good-natured when children, are good-natured when they grow up; and he was always the sweetest tempered, most generous-hearted, boy in the world."

"It is not every one," said Elinor, "who has your passion for dead leaves."

OCTOBER

Anne's object was, not to be in the way of any body, and where the narrow paths across the fields made many separations necessary, to keep with her brother and sister. Her *pleasure* in the walk must arise from the exercise and the day, from the view of the last smiles of the year upon the tawny leaves and withered hedges, and from repeating to herself some few of the thousand poetical descriptions extant of autumn, that season of peculiar and inexhaustible influence on the mind of taste and tenderness, that season which has drawn from every poet, worthy of being read, some attempt at description, or some lines of feeling. She occupied her mind as much as possible in such like musings and quotations; but it was not possible, that when within reach of Captain Wentworth's conversation with either of the Miss Musgroves, she should not try to hear it; yet she caught little very remarkable. It was mere lively chat,—such as any young persons, on an intimate footing, might fall into. He was more engaged with Louisa than with Henrietta. Louisa certainly put more forward for his notice than her sister. This distinction appeared to increase, and there was one speech of Louisa's which struck her. After one of the many praises of the day, which were continually bursting forth, Captain Wentworth added,

"What glorious weather for the Admiral and my sister! They meant to take a long drive this morning; perhaps we may hail them from some of these hills. They talked of coming into this side of the country. I wonder whereabouts they will upset to-day. Oh! it does happen very often, I assure you—but my sister makes nothing of it—she would as lieve be tossed out as not."

"Ah! You make the most of it, I know," cried Louisa, "but if it were really so, I should do just the same in her place. If I loved a man, as she loves the Admiral, I would be always with him, nothing should ever separate us, and I would rather be overturned by him, than driven safely by anybody else."

Persuasion (1818)

OCTOBER 1

"This is always my luck! If there is any thing disagreeable going on, men are always sure to get out of it."

OCTOBER 2

"My fingers," said Elizabeth, "do not move over this instrument in the masterly manner which I see so many women's do. They have not the same force or rapidity, and do not produce the same expression. But then I have always supposed it to be my own fault—because I would not take the trouble of practising."

OCTOBER 3

His looks shewing him not pained, but pleased with this allusion to his situation, she was emboldened to go on; and feeling in herself the right of seniority of mind, she ventured to recommend a larger allowance of prose in his daily study; and on being requested to particularize, mentioned such works of our best moralists, such collections of the finest letters, such memoirs of characters of worth and suffering, as occurred to her at the moment as calculated to rouse and fortify the mind by the highest precepts, and the strongest examples of moral and religious endurances.

OCTOBER 4

PRIDE AND PREJUDICE (1813),
KITTY BENNET AND MR. BENNET

"I am not going to run away, Papa," said Kitty, fretfully; "if *I* should ever go to Brighton, I would behave better than Lydia."

"*You* go to Brighton!—I would not trust you so near it as East Bourne, for fifty pounds! No, Kitty, I have at last learnt to be cautious, and you will feel the effects of it. No officer is ever to enter my house again, nor even to pass through the village. Balls will be absolutely prohibited, unless you stand up with one of your sisters. And you are never to stir out of doors, till you can prove, that you have spent ten minutes of every day in a rational manner."

Kitty, who took all these threats in a serious light, began to cry.

"Well, well," said he, "do not make yourself unhappy. If you are a good girl for the next ten years, I will take you to a review at the end of them."

OCTOBER 5

"My spirit, you know, is pretty independent."

"I wish your heart were independent. That would be enough for me."

"My heart, indeed! What can you have to do with hearts? You men have none of you any hearts."

"If we have not hearts, we have eyes; and they give us torment enough."

OCTOBER 6

"What say you, Mary? for you are a young lady of deep reflection I know, and read great books, and make extracts."

Mary wished to say something very sensible, but knew not how.

OCTOBER 7

"Lizzy," cried her mother, "remember where you are, and do not run on in the wild manner that you are suffered to do at home."

OCTOBER 8

NORTHANGER ABBEY (1818)

Catherine, meanwhile, undisturbed by presentiments of such an evil, or of any evil at all, except that of having but a short set to dance down, enjoyed her usual happiness with Henry Tilney, listening with sparkling eyes to every thing he said; and, in finding him irresistible, becoming so herself.

OCTOBER 9

PRIDE AND PREJUDICE (1813),
ELIZABETH BENNET TO MR. BENNET

"I do not wish to avoid the walk. The distance is nothing, when one has a motive."

OCTOBER 10

SENSE AND SENSIBILITY (1811), MRS. DASHWOOD
TO ELINOR AND MARIANNE DASHWOOD

"I would have every young woman of your condition in life, acquainted with the manners and amusements of London."

OCTOBER 11

PRIDE AND PREJUDICE (1813), MRS. BENNET TO
HER DAUGHTERS AND CHARLOTTE LUCAS

"Those who do not complain are never pitied."

OCTOBER 12

PRIDE AND PREJUDICE (1813),
ELIZABETH BENNET TO MR. DARCY

"There is a stubbornness about me that never can bear to be frightened at the will of others. My courage always rises with every attempt to intimidate me."

OCTOBER 13

SENSE AND SENSIBILITY (1811)

Lady Middleton was equally pleased with Mrs. [Fanny] Dashwood. There was a kind of cold hearted selfishness on both sides, which mutually attracted them; and they sympathised with each other in an insipid propriety of demeanour, and a general want of understanding.

"As far as I have had opportunity of judging, it appears to me that the usual style of letter-writing among women is faultless, except in three particulars."

"And what are they?"

"A general deficiency of subject, a total inattention to stops, and a very frequent ignorance of grammar."

Edward Ferrars was not recommended to their good opinion by any peculiar graces of person or address. He was not handsome, and his manners required intimacy to make them pleasing. He was too diffident to do justice to himself; but when his natural shyness was overcome, his behaviour gave every indication of an open affectionate heart.

OCTOBER 16

"Lizzy, I never gave *you* an account of my wedding, I believe. You were not by, when I told mamma, and the others, all about it. Are not you curious to hear how it was managed?"

"No really," replied Elizabeth; "I think there cannot be too little said on the subject."

"La! You are so strange! But I must tell you how it went off."

OCTOBER 17

No poverty of any kind, except of conversation, appeared—but there, the deficiency was considerable.

OCTOBER 18

"A strong sense of duty is no bad part of a woman's portion."

They parted at last with mutual civility, and possibly a mutual desire of never meeting again.

"I should no more lay it down as a general rule that women write better letters than men, than that they sing better duets, or draw better landscapes. In every power, of which taste is the foundation, excellence is pretty fairly divided between the sexes."

A thousand feelings rushed on Anne, of which this was the most consoling, that it would soon be over. And it was soon over.

OCTOBER 22

LETTER FROM JANE AUSTEN
TO CASSANDRA AUSTEN, 31 MAY 1811

How horrible it is to have so many people killed!—
And what a blessing that one cares for none of them!

OCTOBER 23

PRIDE AND PREJUDICE (1813),
ELIZABETH BENNET TO MRS. GARDINER

"I would have thanked you before, my dear aunt, as
I ought to have done, for your long, kind, satisfactory, detail of particulars; but to say the truth, I was
too cross to write. You supposed more than really
existed. But *now* suppose as much as you chuse; give
a loose to your fancy, indulge your imagination in
every possible flight which the subject will afford,
and unless you belicve me actually married, you cannot greatly err."

OCTOBER 24

NORTHANGER ABBEY (1818),
HENRY TILNEY TO CATHERINE MORLAND

"It is very well worth while to be tormented for two
or three years of one's life, for the sake of being able
to read all the rest of it."

OCTOBER 25

PRIDE AND PREJUDICE (1813), ELIZABETH BENNET
TO CHARLOTTE LUCAS, ON MR. DARCY

"I could easily forgive *his* pride, if he had not mortified *mine*."

OCTOBER 26

LETTER FROM JANE AUSTEN TO
CASSANDRA AUSTEN, 26 OCTOBER 1813

I am not at all in a humour for writing; I must write on till I am.

OCTOBER 27

MANSFIELD PARK (1814), MARY CRAWFORD TO
EDMUND BERTRAM, FANNY PRICE, AND OTHERS

"Certainly, my home at my uncle's brought me acquainted with a circle of admirals. Of *Rears*, and *Vices*, I saw enough. Now, do not be suspecting me of a pun, I entreat."

OCTOBER 28

LETTER FROM JANE AUSTEN TO
CASSANDRA AUSTEN, 27–28 OCTOBER 1798

Mrs Hall of Sherbourn was brought to bed yesterday

of a dead child, some weeks before she expected, oweing to a fright.—I suppose she happened unawares to look at her husband.

OCTOBER 29

LETTER FROM JANE AUSTEN TO
FANNY KNIGHT, 18–20 NOVEMBER 1814

And now, my dear Fanny, having written so much on one side of the question, I shall turn round & entreat you not to commit yourself farther, & not to think of accepting him unless you really do like him. Anything is to be preferred or endured rather than marrying without Affection; and if his deficiencies of Manner &c &c strike you more than all his good qualities, if you continue to think strongly of them, give him up at once.—Things are now in such a state, that you must resolve upon one or the other, either to allow him to go on as he has done, or whenever you are together behave with a coldness which may convince him that he has been deceiving himself.—I have no doubt of his suffering a good deal for a time, a great deal, when he feels that he must give you up;—but it is no creed of mine, as you must be well aware, that such sort of Disappointments kill anybody.

"Pardon me for interrupting you, Madam," cried Mr. Collins; "but if she is really headstrong and foolish, I know not whether she would altogether be a very desirable wife to a man in my situation, who naturally looks for happiness in the marriage state. If therefore she actually persists in rejecting my suit, perhaps it were better not to force her into accepting me, because if liable to such defects of temper, she could not contribute much to my felicity."

"Sir, you quite misunderstand me," said Mrs. Bennet, alarmed. "Lizzy is only headstrong in such matters as these. In every thing else she is as good natured a girl as ever lived."

"Ah, mother! how do you do?" said he, giving her a hearty shake of the hand: "where did you get that quiz of a hat, it makes you look like an old witch?"

NOVEMBER

Yes, novels;—for I will not adopt that ungenerous and impolitic custom so common with novel writers, of degrading by their contemptuous censure the very performances, to the number of which they are themselves adding—joining with their greatest enemies in bestowing the harshest epithets on such works, and scarcely ever permitting them to be read by their own heroine, who, if she accidentally take up a novel, is sure to turn over its insipid pages with disgust. Alas! if the heroine of one novel be not patronized by the heroine of another, from whom can she expect protection and regard? I cannot approve of it. Let us leave it to the Reviewers to abuse such effusions of fancy at their leisure, and over every new novel to talk in threadbare strains of the trash with which the press now groans. Let us not desert one another; we are an injured body. Although our productions have afforded more extensive and unaffected pleasure than those of any other literary corporation in the world, no species of composition has been so much decried. From pride, ignorance, or fashion, our foes are almost as many as our readers. And while the abilities of the nine-hundredth abridger of the History of England, or of the man who collects and publishes in a volume some dozen lines of Milton, Pope, and Prior, with a paper from the Spectator, and a chapter from Sterne, are eulogized by a thousand pens,—there seems almost a general wish of decrying the capacity and undervaluing the labour of the novelist, and of slighting the performances which have only genius, wit, and taste to recommend them. "I am no novel reader—I seldom look into novels—Do not imagine that *I* often read novels—It is really very well for a novel."—Such is the common cant.—"And what are you reading, Miss——?" "Oh! it is only a novel!" replies the young lady; while she lays down her book with affected indifference, or momentary shame.—"It is only Cecilia, or Camilla, or Belinda;" or, in short, only some work in which the greatest powers of the mind are displayed, in which the most thorough knowledge of human nature, the happiest delineation of its varieties, the liveliest effusions of wit and humour are conveyed to the world in the best chosen language.

Northanger Abbey (1818)

"My first wish for all, whom I am interested in, is that they should be firm. If Louisa Musgrove would be beautiful and happy in her November of life, she will cherish all her present powers of mind."

Mrs. Allen was one of that numerous class of females, whose society can raise no other emotion than surprise at there being any men in the world who could like them well enough to marry them. She had neither beauty, genius, accomplishment, nor manner. The air of a gentlewoman, a great deal of quiet, inactive good temper, and a trifling turn of mind, were all that could account for her being the choice of a sensible, intelligent man, like Mr. Allen. In one respect she was admirably fitted to introduce a young lady into public, being as fond of going everywhere and seeing every thing herself as any young lady could be. Dress was her passion. She had a most harmless delight in being fine; and our heroine's entrée into life could not take place till after three or four days had been spent in learning what was mostly worn, and her chaperon was provided with a dress of the newest fashion.

NOVEMBER 3

SANDITON (1817), SIR EDWARD DENHAM
AND CHARLOTTE HEYWOOD

"I am no indiscriminate novel-reader. The mere trash of the common circulating library, I hold in the highest contempt. You will never hear me advocating those puerile emanations which detail nothing but discordant principles incapable of amalgamation, or those vapid tissues of ordinary occurrences from which no useful deductions can be drawn.—In vain may we put them into a literary alembic;—we distil nothing which can add to science.—You understand me I am sure?"

"I am not quite certain that I do.—But if you will describe the sort of novels which you *do* approve, I dare say it will give me a clearer idea."

NOVEMBER 4

LADY SUSAN (C. 1794–1805),
LADY SUSAN VERNON TO MRS. JOHNSON

I trust I shall be able to make my story as good as her's.—If I am vain of any thing, it is of my eloquence. Consideration & Esteem as surely follow command of Language, as Admiration waits on Beauty.

NOVEMBER 5

NORTHANGER ABBEY (1818)

Henry suffered the subject to decline, and by an easy transition from a piece of rocky fragment and the withered oak which he had placed near its summit, to oaks in general, to forests, the inclosure of them, waste lands, crown lands and government, he shortly found himself arrived at politics; and from politics, it was an easy step to silence.

NOVEMBER 6

LETTER FROM JANE AUSTEN TO
CASSANDRA AUSTEN, 6–7 NOVEMBER 1813

By the bye, as I must leave off being young, I find many Douceurs in being a sort of Chaperon for I am put on the Sofa near the Fire & can drink as much wine as I like.

NOVEMBER 7

It would be mortifying to the feelings of many ladies, could they be made to understand how little the heart of man is affected by what is costly or new in their attire; how little it is biassed by the texture of their muslin, and how unsusceptible of peculiar tenderness towards the spotted, the sprigged, the mull or the jackonet. Woman is fine for her own satisfaction alone. No man will admire her the more, no woman will like her the better for it. Neatness and fashion are enough for the former, and a something of shabbiness or impropriety will be most endearing to the latter.

NOVEMBER 8

The Tables are come, & give general contentment. I had not expected that they would so perfectly suit the fancy of us all three, or that we should so well agree in the disposition of them; but nothing except their own surface can have been smoother;— The two ends put together form our constant Table for everything, & the centre peice stands exceedingly well under the glass; holds a great deal most commodiously, without looking awkwardly.—They are both covered with green baize & send their best Love.

NOVEMBER 9

"Yes, yes, if you please, no reference to examples in books. Men have had every advantage of us in telling their own story. Education has been theirs in so much higher a degree; the pen has been in their hands. I will not allow books to prove any thing."

"But how shall we prove any thing?"

"We never shall. We never can expect to prove any thing upon such a point. It is a difference of opinion which does not admit of proof. We each begin probably with a little bias towards our own sex, and upon that bias build every circumstance in favour of it which has occurred within our own circle; many of which circumstances (perhaps those very cases which strike us the most) may be precisely such as cannot be brought forward without betraying a confidence, or in some respect saying what should not be said."

MANSFIELD PARK (1814),

ON MRS. NORRIS AND MARIA BERTRAM

Shut up together with little society, on one side no affection, on the other, no judgment, it may be reasonably supposed that their tempers became their mutual punishment.

NOVEMBER 11

NORTHANGER ABBEY (1818),

CATHERINE MORLAND AND HENRY TILNEY

"But you never read novels, I dare say?"

"Why not?"

"Because they are not clever enough for you—gentlemen read better books."

"The person, be it gentleman or lady, who has not pleasure in a good novel, must be intolerably stupid. I have read all Mrs. Radcliffe's works, and most of them with great pleasure. The Mysteries of Udolpho, when I had once begun it, I could not lay down again;—I remember finishing it in two days—my hair standing on end the whole time."

NOVEMBER 12

SENSE AND SENSIBILITY (1811)

John Dashwood had not much to say for himself that was worth hearing, and his wife had still less. But there was no peculiar disgrace in this, for it was very much the case with the chief of their visitors, who almost all laboured under one or other of these disqualifications for being agreeable—Want of sense, either natural or improved—want of elegance—want of spirits—or want of temper.

NOVEMBER 13

LESLEY CASTLE (C. 1792), MISS MARGARET LESLEY
TO MISS CHARLOTTE LUTTERELL

We are handsome my dear Charlotte, very handsome and the greatest of our Perfections is, that we are entirely insensible of them ourselves.

NOVEMBER 14

PERSUASION (1818), MRS. CROFT
TO ADMIRAL CROFT

"My dear admiral, that post!—we shall certainly take that post."

But by coolly giving the reins a better direction

herself, they happily passed the danger; and by once afterwards judiciously putting out her hand, they neither fell into a rut, nor ran foul of a dung-cart; and Anne, with some amusement at their style of driving, which she imagined no bad representation of the general guidance of their affairs, found herself safely deposited by them at the cottage.

NOVEMBER 15

HENRY AND ELIZA (C. 1788–89), ELIZA'S THOUGHTS

But scarcely was she provided with the above-mentioned necessaries, than she began to find herself rather hungry, and had reason to think, by their biting off two of her fingers, that her Children were much in the same situation.

NOVEMBER 16

NORTHANGER ABBEY (1818),
HENRY TILNEY AND ELEANOR TILNEY

"What am I to do?"

"You know what you ought to do. Clear your character handsomely before her. Tell her that you think very highly of the understanding of women."

"Miss Morland, I think very highly of the understanding of all the women in the world—especially of those—whoever they may be—with whom I happen to be in company."

"That is not enough. Be more serious."

"Miss Morland, no one can think more highly of the understanding of women than I do. In my opinion, nature has given them so much, that they never find it necessary to use more than half."

"We shall get nothing more serious from him now, Miss Morland. He is not in a sober mood. But I do assure you that he must be entirely misunderstood, if he can ever appear to say an unjust thing of any woman at all, or an unkind one of me."

NOVEMBER 17

LETTER FROM JANE AUSTEN TO
CASSANDRA AUSTEN, 17–18 NOVEMBER 1798

Mrs. Portman is not much admired in Dorsetshire; the good-natured world, as usual, extolled her beauty so highly, that all the neighbourhood have had the pleasure of being disappointed.

NOVEMBER 18

LETTER FROM JANE AUSTEN TO
CASSANDRA AUSTEN, 17–18 NOVEMBER 1798

My mother desires me to tell you that I am a very

good housekeeper, which I have no reluctance in doing, because I really think it my peculiar excellence,
and for this reason—I always take care to provide
such things as please my own appetite, which I consider as the chief merit in housekeeping.

"A young man of eighteen is not in general so ear-
nestly bent on being busy as to resist the solicita-
tions of his friends to do nothing."

"How differently we feel!" cried Fanny. "To me,
the sound of *Mr.* Bertram is so cold and nothing-
meaning—so entirely without warmth or character!
—It just stands for a gentleman, and that's all. But
there is nobleness in the name of Edmund. It is a
name of heroism and renown—of kings, princes,
and knights; and seems to breathe the spirit of chiv-
alry and warm affections."

CATHARINE, OR THE BOWER (C. 1792),
CATHARINE (OR KITTY) PERCIVAL (OR PETERSON)
AND CAMILLA STANLEY

"For my own part, if a book is well written, I always find it too short."

"So do I, only I get tired of it before it is finished."

NOVEMBER 22

PRIDE AND PREJUDICE (1813)

Elizabeth now began to revive. But not long was the interval of tranquillity; for when supper was over, singing was talked of, and she had the mortification of seeing Mary, after very little entreaty, preparing to oblige the company. By many significant looks and silent entreaties, did she endeavour to prevent such a proof of complaisance,—but in vain; Mary would not understand them; such an opportunity of exhibiting was delightful to her, and she began her song. Elizabeth's eyes were fixed on her with most painful sensations; and she watched her progress through the several stanzas with an impatience which was very ill rewarded at their close; for Mary, on receiving amongst the thanks of the table, the hint of a hope that she might be prevailed on to favour them again, after the pause of half a minute began another. Mary's powers were by no means fitted for such a display; her voice was weak, and her manner affected.—Elizabeth was in agonies. She looked at Jane, to see how she bore it; but Jane was very composedly talking to Bingley. She looked at his two sisters, and saw them making signs of derision at each other, and at Darcy, who continued however impenetrably grave. She looked at her father to entreat his interference, lest Mary should be singing all night. He took the hint, and when Mary had finished her second song, said aloud,

"That will do extremely well, child. You have delighted us long enough. Let the other young ladies have time to exhibit."

Mary, though pretending not to hear, was somewhat disconcerted; and Elizabeth sorry for her, and sorry for her father's speech, was afraid her anxiety had done no good.

NOVEMBER 23

SENSE AND SENSIBILITY (1811), MRS. JENNINGS TO ELINOR DASHWOOD, ON MR. WILLOUGHBY

"Well, said I, all I can say is, that if it is true, he has used a young lady of my acquaintance abominably ill, and I wish with all my soul his wife may plague his heart out."

NOVEMBER 24

I make no apologies for my heroine's vanity.—If there are young ladies in the world at her time of life, more dull of fancy and more careless of pleasing, I know them not, and never wish to know them.

NOVEMBER 25

LETTER FROM JANE AUSTEN TO
CASSANDRA AUSTEN, 25 NOVEMBER 1798

I shall not write again for many days; perhaps a little repose may restore my regard for a pen.

NOVEMBER 26

SENSE AND SENSIBILITY (1811),
MRS. DASHWOOD TO SIR JOHN MIDDLETON

"I do not believe," said Mrs. Dashwood, with a good humoured smile, "that Mr. Willoughby will be incommoded by the attempts of either of *my* daughters towards what you call *catching him*. It is not an employment to which they have been brought up. Men are very safe with us, let them be ever so rich."

"You are then resolved to have him?"

"I have said no such thing. I am only resolved to act in that manner, which will, in my own opinion, constitute my happiness, without reference to *you*, or to any person so wholly unconnected with me."

"It is well. You refuse, then, to oblige me. You refuse to obey the claims of duty, honour, and gratitude. You are determined to ruin him in the opinion of all his friends, and make him the contempt of the world."

"Neither duty, nor honour, nor gratitude," replied Elizabeth, "have any possible claim on me, in the present instance. No principle of either, would be violated by my marriage with Mr. Darcy. And with regard to the resentment of his family, or the indignation of the world, if the former *were* excited by his marrying me, it would not give me one moment's concern—and the world in general would have too much sense to join in the scorn."

"And this is your real opinion! This is your final resolve! Very well. I shall now know how to act. Do not imagine, Miss Bennet, that your ambition will ever be gratified. I came to try you. I hoped to find you reasonable; but depend upon it I will carry my point."

In this manner Lady Catherine talked on, till they were at the door of the carriage, when turning hastily round, she added,

"I take no leave of you, Miss Bennet. I send no compliments to your mother. You deserve no such attention. I am most seriously displeased."

NOVEMBER 28

EMMA (1816), EMMA WOODHOUSE
TO HARRIET SMITH

"I shall not be a poor old maid; and it is poverty only which makes celibacy contemptible to a generous public! A single woman, with a very narrow income, must be a ridiculous, disagreeable, old maid! the proper sport of boys and girls; but a single woman, of good fortune, is always respectable, and may be as sensible and pleasant as anybody else."

NOVEMBER 29

MANSFIELD PARK (1814), FANNY PRICE TO HERSELF

"Oh! write, write. Finish it at once. Let there be an end of this suspense. Fix, commit, condemn yourself."

Tho' I like praise as well as anybody, I like what Edward calls *Pewter* too.

DECEMBER

"Come, Darcy," said he, "I must have you dance. I hate to see you standing about by yourself in this stupid manner. You had much better dance."

"I certainly shall not. You know how I detest it, unless I am particularly acquainted with my partner. At such an assembly as this, it would be insupportable. Your sisters are engaged, and there is not another woman in the room, whom it would not be a punishment to me to stand up with."

"I would not be so fastidious as you are," cried Bingley, "for a kingdom! Upon my honour, I never met with so many pleasant girls in my life, as I have this evening; and there are several of them you see uncommonly pretty."

"*You* are dancing with the only handsome girl in the room," said Mr. Darcy, looking at the eldest Miss Bennet.

"Oh! she is the most beautiful creature I ever beheld! But there is one of her sisters sitting down just behind you, who is very pretty, and I dare say, very agreeable. Do let me ask my partner to introduce you."

"Which do you mean?" and turning round, he looked for a moment at Elizabeth, till catching her eye, he withdrew his own and coldly said, "She is tolerable; but not handsome enough to tempt *me*; and I am in no humour at present to give consequence to young ladies who are slighted by other men. You had better return to your partner and enjoy her smiles, for you are wasting your time with me."

Mr. Bingley followed his advice. Mr. Darcy walked off; and Elizabeth remained with no very cordial feelings towards him. She told the story however with great spirit among her friends; for she had a lively, playful disposition, which delighted in any thing ridiculous.

Pride and Prejudice (1813),
Mr. Bingley and Mr. Darcy

DECEMBER 1

LETTER FROM JANE AUSTEN TO
CASSANDRA AUSTEN, 1–2 DECEMBER 1798

I have made myself two or three caps to wear of evenings since I came home, and they save me a world of torment as to hairdressing.

DECEMBER 2

MANSFIELD PARK (1814),
MARY CRAWFORD TO FANNY PRICE

"The profession, either navy or army, is its own justification. It has every thing in its favour; heroism, danger, bustle, fashion. Soldiers and sailors are always acceptable in society. Nobody can wonder that men are soldiers and sailors."

DECEMBER 3

EMMA (1816), MR. WOODHOUSE AND
EMMA WOODHOUSE

"And he is a very clever boy, indeed. They are all remarkably clever; and they have so many pretty ways. They will come and stand by my chair, and say, 'Grandpapa, can you give me a bit of string?' and once Henry asked me for a knife, but I told him knives were only made for grandpapas. I think their father is too rough with them very often."

"He appears rough to you," said Emma, "because you are so very gentle yourself; but if you could compare him with other papas, you would not think him rough. He wishes his boys to be active and hardy; and if they misbehave, can give them a sharp word now and then; but he is an affectionate father—certainly Mr. John Knightley is an affectionate father. The children are all fond of him."

"And then their uncle comes in, and tosses them up to the ceiling in a very frightful way!"

"But they like it, papa; there is nothing they like so much. It is such enjoyment to them, that if their uncle did not lay down the rule of their taking turns, which ever began would never give way to the other."

"Well, I cannot understand it."

"That is the case with us all, papa. One half of the world cannot understand the pleasures of the other."

DECEMBER 4

MANSFIELD PARK (1814),
MARIA BERTRAM'S THOUGHTS

It was a gloomy prospect, and all that she could do was throw a mist over it, and hope when the mist cleared away, she should see something else.

DECEMBER 5

CATHARINE, OR THE BOWER (C. 1792),
CATHARINE (OR KITTY) PERCIVAL (OR PETERSON)
AND CAMILLA STANLEY

"I am in love with every handsome Man I see."

"That is just like me—*I* am always in love with every handsome Man in the World."

"There you outdo me replied Catherine for I am only in love with those I *do* see."

DECEMBER 6

THE HISTORY OF ENGLAND (C. 1791)

Henry the 6th. I cannot say much for this Monarch's Sense—Nor would I if I could, for he was a Lancastrian. I suppose you know all about the Wars between him and the Duke of York who was of the right side; if you do not, you had better read some other History.

DECEMBER 7

PERSUASION (1818), ANNE ELLIOT'S THOUGHTS

The dread of a future war [was] all that could dim her sunshine.

Poor Edward muttered something, but what it was, nobody knew, not even himself.

"But I hate to hear you talking so, like a fine gentleman, and as if women were all fine ladies, instead of rational creatures. We none of us expect to be in smooth water all our days."

"Ah! my dear," said the admiral, "when he has got a wife, he will sing a different tune. When he is married, if we have the good luck to live to another war, we shall see him do as you and I, and a great many others, have done. We shall have him very thankful to any body that will bring him his wife."

"Ay, that we shall."

"Now I have done," cried Captain Wentworth— "When once married people begin to attack me with, 'Oh! you will think very differently, when you are married.' I can only say, 'No, I shall not;' and then they say again, 'Yes, you will,' and there is an end of it."

Whether the torments of absence were softened by a clandestine correspondence, let us not inquire.

DECEMBER 11

LETTER FROM JANE AUSTEN TO
JAMES STANIER CLARKE, 11 DECEMBER 1815

I am quite honoured by your thinking me capable of drawing such a Clergyman as you gave the sketch of in your note of Nov: 16. But I assure you I am *not*. The comic part of the Character I might be equal to, but not the Good, the Enthusiastic, the Literary. Such a Man's Conversation must at times be on subjects of Science & Philosophy of which I know nothing—or at least be occasionally abundant in quotations & allusions which a Woman, who like me, knows only her own Mother-tongue & has read very little in that, would be totally without the power of giving.—A Classical Education, or at any rate, a very extensive acquaintance with English Literature, Ancient & Modern, appears to me quite Indispensable for the person who w^d do any justice to your Clergyman— And I think I may boast myself to be, with all possible Vanity, the most unlearned, & uninformed Female who ever dared to be an Authoress.

DECEMBER 12

She saw no reason against their being happy. Louisa had fine naval fervour to begin with, and they would soon grow more alike. He would gain cheerfulness; and she would learn to be an enthusiast for Scott and Lord Byron; nay, that was probably learnt already; of course they had fallen in love over poetry. The idea of Louisa Musgrove turned into a person of literary taste, and sentimental reflection, was amusing, but she had no doubt of its being so. The day at Lyme, the fall from the Cobb, might influence her health, her nerves, her courage, her character to the end of her life, as thoroughly as it appeared to have influenced her fate.

DECEMBER 13

SENSE AND SENSIBILITY (1811)

The night was cold and stormy. The wind roared round the house, and the rain beat against the windows; but Elinor, all happiness within, regarded it not.

"Yes, here I am, Sophia, quite ready to make a foolish match. Any body between fifteen and thirty may have me for asking. A little beauty, and a few smiles, and a few compliments to the navy, and I am a lost man. Should not this be enough for a sailor, who has had no society among women to make him nice?"

He said it, she knew, to be contradicted. His bright, proud eye spoke the happy conviction that he was nice; and Anne Elliot was not out of his thoughts, when he more seriously described the woman he should wish to meet with. "A strong mind, with sweetness of manner," made the first and the last of the description.

"This is the woman I want," said he, "Something a little inferior I shall of course put up with, but it must not be much. If I am a fool, I shall be a fool indeed, for I have thought on the subject more than most men."

"Nobody is healthy in London, nobody can be."

By the bye, my dear Edward, I am quite concerned for the loss your Mother mentions in her Letter; two Chapters & a half to be missing is monstrous! It is well that *I* have not been at Steventon lately, & therefore cannot be suspected of purloining them;—two strong twigs & a half towards a Nest of my own, would have been something.—I do not think however that any theft of that sort would be really very useful to me. What should I do with your strong, manly, spirited Sketches, full of variety & Glow?— How could I possibly join them on to the little bit (two Inches wide) of Ivory on which I work with so fine a Brush, as produces little effect after much labour?

DECEMBER 17

PRIDE AND PREJUDICE (1813),
JANE BENNET AND ELIZABETH BENNET

"I was very much flattered by his asking me to dance a second time. I did not expect such a compliment."

"Did not you? *I* did for you. But that is one great difference between us. Compliments always take *you* by surprise, and *me* never."

DECEMBER 18

My dear Cassandra

Your letter came quite as soon as I expected, and so your letters will always do, because I have made it a rule not to expect them till they come, in which I think I consult the ease of us both.

DECEMBER 19

I have received a very civil note from Mrs Martin requesting my name as a Subscriber to her Library which opens the 14th of January, & my name, or rather Yours is accordingly given. My Mother finds the Money.—Mary subscribes too, which I am glad of, but hardly expected.—As an inducement to subscribe Mrs Martin tells us that her Collection is not to consist only of Novels, but of every kind of Literature &c &c—She might have spared this pretension to *our* family, who are great Novel-readers & not ashamed of being so;—but it was necessary I suppose to the self-consequence of half her Subscribers.

DECEMBER 20

Such were her propensities—her abilities were quite as extraordinary. She never could learn or understand any thing before she was taught; and sometimes not even then, for she was often inattentive, and occasionally stupid. Her mother was three months in teaching her only to repeat the "Beggar's Petition;" and after all, her next sister, Sally, could say it better than she did. Not that Catherine was always stupid,—by no means; she learnt the fable of "The Hare and many Friends," as quickly as any girl in England.

DECEMBER 21

He was, at that time, a remarkably fine young man, with a great deal of intelligence, spirit and brilliancy; and Anne an extremely pretty girl, with gentleness, modesty, taste, and feeling.—Half the sum of attraction, on either side, might have been enough, for he had nothing to do, and she had hardly any body to love; but the encounter of such lavish recommendations could not fail. They were gradually acquainted, and when acquainted, rapidly and deeply in love. It would be difficult to say which had seen highest perfection in the other, or which had been the happiest; she, in receiving his declarations and proposals, or he in having them accepted.

"Some people imagine that there can be no accommodations, no space in a cottage; but this is all a mistake. I was last month at my friend Elliott's near Dartford. Lady Elliott wished to give a dance. 'But how can it be done?' said she; 'my dear Ferrars, do tell me how it is to be managed. There is not a room in this cottage that will hold ten couple, and where can the supper be?' *I* immediately saw that there could be no difficulty in it, so I said, 'My dear Lady Elliott, do not be uneasy. The dining parlour will admit eighteen couple with ease; card-tables may be placed in the drawing-room; the library may be open for tea and other refreshments; and let the supper be set out in the saloon.' Lady Elliott was delighted with the thought. We measured the dining-room, and found it would hold exactly eighteen couple, and the affair was arranged precisely after my plan. So that, in fact, you see, if people do but know how to set about it, every comfort may be as well enjoyed in a cottage as in the most spacious dwelling."

Elinor agreed to it all, for she did not think he deserved the compliment of rational opposition.

DECEMBER 23

MANSFIELD PARK (1814)

The indignities of stupidity, and the disappointments of selfish passion, can excite little pity.

DECEMBER 24

LETTER FROM JANE AUSTEN TO
CASSANDRA AUSTEN, 24–26 DECEMBER 1798

You deserve a longer letter than this; but it is my unhappy fate seldom to treat people so well as they deserve.

DECEMBER 25

EMMA (1816), MR. ELTON AND MR. JOHN KNIGHTLEY

"Christmas weather," observed Mr. Elton. "Quite seasonable; and extremely fortunate we may think ourselves that it did not begin yesterday, and prevent this day's party, which it might very possibly have done, for Mr. Woodhouse would hardly have ventured had there been much snow on the ground;

but now it is of no consequence. This is quite the season indeed for friendly meetings. At Christmas every body invites their friends about them, and people think little of even the worst weather. I was snowed up at a friend's house once for a week. Nothing could be pleasanter. I went for only one night, and could not get away till that very day se'nnight."

Mr. John Knightley looked as if he did not comprehend the pleasure, but said only, coolly,

"I cannot wish to be snowed up a week at Randalls."

DECEMBER 26

SANDITON (1817), CHARLOTTE HEYWOOD'S
THOUGHTS ON SIR EDWARD DENHAM

She could not but think him a man of feeling—till he began to stagger her by the number of his quotations, and the bewilderment of some of his sentences.

DECEMBER 27

SENSE AND SENSIBILITY (1811), MARIANNE AND
ELINOR DASHWOOD, ON MR. WILLOUGHBY

Marianne's lips quivered, and she repeated the word "Selfish?" in a tone that implied—"do you really think him selfish?"

"The whole of his behaviour," replied Elinor,

"from the beginning to the end of the affair, has been grounded on selfishness. It was selfishness which first made him sport with your affections; which afterwards, when his own were engaged, made him delay the confession of it, and which finally carried him from Barton. His own enjoyment, or his own ease, was, in every particular, his ruling principle."

"It is very true. *My* happiness never was his object."

DECEMBER 28

Frank Churchill came back again; and if he kept his father's dinner waiting, it was not known at Hartfield; for Mrs. Weston was too anxious for his being a favourite with Mr. Woodhouse, to betray any imperfection which could be concealed.

He came back, had had his hair cut, and laughed at himself with a very good grace, but without seeming really at all ashamed of what he had done. He had no reason to wish his hair longer, to conceal any confusion of face; no reason to wish the money unspent, to improve his spirits. He was quite as undaunted and as lively as ever; and after seeing him, Emma thus moralized to herself:—

"I do not know whether it ought to be so, but certainly silly things do cease to be silly if they are done by sensible people in an impudent way. Wickedness is always wickedness, but folly is not always folly.—It depends upon the character of those who handle it."

DECEMBER 29

SENSE AND SENSIBILITY (1811)

Marianne Dashwood was born to an extraordinary fate. She was born to discover the falsehood of her own opinions, and to counteract, by her conduct, her most favourite maxims.

DECEMBER 30

MANSFIELD PARK (1814)

Let other pens dwell on guilt and misery. I quit such odious subjects as soon as I can, impatient to restore every body, not greatly in fault themselves, to tolerable comfort, and to have done with all the rest.

DECEMBER 31

EMMA (1816), FRANK CHURCHILL TO EMMA WOOD-HOUSE

"Of all horrid things, leave-taking is the worst."

Index of Sources

February 29, March 9, March 16, March 26, April 12, April 23, May 9, May 11, May 18, May 24, June 11, June 26, July 7, July 9, July 19, July 25, August 8, August 10, August 15, August 21, August 24, August 27, August 30, September 3, September 10, September 19, September 22, September 24, October 27, November 10, November 20, November 29, December 2, December 4, December 23, December 30

Northanger Abbey, January 1, January 8, January 16, January 18, January 22, February 15, February 18, March 6, March 10, March 31, April 6, April 7, May 7, May 13, May 20, June 7, June 21, June 25, *July*, July 3, July 20, July 22, July 30, August 5, August 31, September 11, September 17, October 5, October 8, October 14, October 20, October 24, October 31, *November*, November 2, November 5, November 7, November 11, November 16, December 10, December 20

Persuasion, January 3, January 30, February 5, February 12, February 21, *March*, March 11, March 14, March 25, March 27, April 3, April 14, April 15, April 19, April 22, April 25, April 26, April 28, April 30, May 3, May 6, May 15, May 25, May 27, June 4, June 6, June 9, June 13, June 17, June 19, June 23, June 29, July 4, July 8, July 12, July 17, July 23, July 26, July 28, August 9, August 12, September 4, September 6, *October*, October 1, October 3, October 18, October 21, November 1, November 9, November 14, December 7, December 9, December 12, December 14, December 21

Pride and Prejudice, *January*, January 7, January 15, January 25, January 27, February 3, February 16, February 22, March 5, March 22, *April*, April 4, April 21, April 24, April 29, *May*, May 2, May 5, May 14, May 19, May 21, May 22, May 28, May 30, *June*, June 18, June 30, July 6, July 13, July 16, July 27, July 29, July 31, *August*, August 7, August 11, August 16, August 17, August 18, August 19, August 20, August 22, August 25, August 26, August 28, September 8, September 12, September 13, September 21, September 26, September 27, September 29, October 2, October 4, October 6, October 7,

October 9, October 11, October 12, October 16, October 19, October 23, October 25, October 30, November 22, November 27, *December*, December 17

Sanditon, January 17, January 20, January 21, February 1, February 10, March 4, March 8, March 17, March 18, May 16, September 14, September 23, November 3, November 24, December 26

Sense and Sensibility, January 4, January 12, January 28, *February*, February 4, February 6, February 11, February 14, February 24, February 28, March 1, March 3, March 7, March 15, March 28, April 10, April 27, May 4, May 12, May 23, May 29, June 1, June 12, June 14, June 27, July 10, July 21, August 13, August 29, September 7, September 28, September 30, October 10, October 13, October 15, October 17, November 12, November 19, November 23, November 26, December 8, December 13, December 22, December 27, December 29

The Watsons, January 13, March 21, May 8, June 2, August 2

Note on the Text

Excerpts from Austen's novels are quoted, by permission, from *The Cambridge Edition of the Works of Jane Austen*, Janet Todd, general editor, 8 vols. It is the standard edition of Austen's works: her *Juvenilia* (2006), edited by Peter Sabor; *Sense and Sensibility* (2006), edited by Edward Copeland; *Pride and Prejudice* (2006), edited by Pat Rogers; *Mansfield Park* (2005), edited by John Wiltshire; *Emma* (2005), edited by Richard Cronin and Dorothy McMillan; *Northanger Abbey* (2006), edited by Barbara M. Benedict and Deirdre Le Faye; *Persuasion* (2006), edited by Janet Todd and Antje Blank; and *Later Manuscripts* (2008), edited by Janet Todd and Linda Bree.

Quotations from Austen's letters are taken from the only complete edition, *Jane Austen's Letters* (2011), edited by Deirdre Le Faye, now in its fourth edition from Oxford University Press. I am very grateful to Oxford for granting permission to publish them here.

Acknowledgments

Much gratitude to all the Janeites, especially those on Facebook, who offered ideas by the dozen about which quotations deserved inclusion. Cherished friends from the Jane Austen Society of North America, and Austen societies worldwide, know that this book could easily be *A Decade of Jane Austen*. A shout-out, too, to the roller derby girls in my life, who propel forward my love of women's empowerment, snarky wit, and top speed.

I've depended on the astonishing generosity and nobleness of conduct of many scholars and editors. I owe a debt to Peter Sabor, Deidre Lynch, and Michael Gorra for their advice on, and support of, this book. Christine Schwab's keen eye made it better, and my fabulous editor Maggie Hivnor shaped it in ways large and small.

My fine family—with its fortunate heads, arms, and legs enough—deserves endless appreciation, especially my mother, Sharon Looser, for starting it all by nudging me to read Austen in my teens. I thank her, in her own particular argot, "very moochly."

I'm grateful to my father, LeRoy Looser, for inculcating a love of research and a zest for trying new things. He first picked up *Pride and Prejudice* three years ago, in his late seventies. I treasure the day he told me, his only daughter, "I just got to the part where Lydia's going to Brighton with Mrs. Forster. I don't know what kind of trouble she's going to get in down there. Don't tell me."

This book takes its inspiration from my overly blunt, Austen-skeptical teen sons. Carl Justice, when told about *The Daily Jane Austen*, said, "That's ridiculous. Why do people need a Jane Austen quote book? Can't they just read the novels?" His younger brother, Lowell Justice, was clearly channeling his inner Mr. Bingley. He countered, "Mom, that's cool. Sounds awesome!" I love them both in equal measure.

Thanks, finally, to George Justice, my well-looking, if a little weather-beaten, Admiral. Let us never fall into a rut or run foul of a dung cart.